Harlin Bentley

Berkley's Bastards Book 4

KATHI S. BARTON

World Castle Publishing, LLC
Pensacola, Florida
Copyright © 2023 Kathi S. Barton
Paperback ISBN: 9798891260368
eBook ISBN: 9798891260375
First Edition World Castle Publishing, LLC, August 21, 2023
http://www.worldcastlepublishing.com
Licensing Notes
Cover: Karen Fuller
Editor: Karen Fuller

Chapter 1

Harlin wasn't sure that he hadn't dialed the wrong number again. Telling the man on the other end of the call his name, he waited for a few seconds before speaking again. He normally didn't care to fill in where there was silence, but he had to speak to this person before he could simply move on.

"A man by the name of Caleb Anderson was trying to contact me. However, the number that I was given was for an attorney by the name of Fowler. I'm not entirely sure what an attorney would want with me." The person at the other end told him that was the name of the attorney that was trying to contact the men that had been sired by a man by the name of Berkley. "Yeah, that's the man's name on my birth certificate. He and my mom were an item for a long time. I'm not sure that they'd be called an item, but it worked for the two of them. Then he had her send me off to military school when I was about eight. From there, I avoided them both as much as possible. Is this about the books? Or does this have to do with something else with you trying to contact me?"

"Books? I never heard anything about a book from...I, as well as a few other men, have the same sire as you do. Just after his mother passed away, Caleb found out about the others that had been raped by this man, and he's looking for them. It was his mom's dying wish. I do know that your mother is still alive. But other than that, I've no idea how I was to contact her nor you, for that matter, other than to have had an attorney looking for you. You'd be the only one so far that has their parent still living. By the way, my name is Joey Phillips." Harlin said that he didn't have much in the way of contact with her. That she'd been in an asylum for the last few years. "I'm sorry to hear that. But I'm a half-brother to you as well as Caleb and a few other men that we're trying to contact."

"Why? I don't want to sound crass or anything, but I mean, it's been decades since I was born. Why are you just now getting around to it?" Harlin knew he was being harsh, but he wasn't in the mood to bring up shit after all this time. "I'm not sure what you think can come of this, but I'm happy with the way things are for me. Berkley is dead and not knocking me around anymore, nor my mom. Which, I'm sure, you know all about his death. My mom... well, she's safe where she is now that he's not in her life and leaving her alone. Things that might have been better for the two of us had he done that. But he didn't. He knew exactly what to say or do to have her begging him to stay with her."

"None of the others of us that I've been able to speak to knew Berkley other than the fact that he had raped our mothers and left them. No personal contact at all, as far as we can tell. As for the book, I'm assuming that it has something to do with your life with him. Or perhaps mention of any of the other women that he raped. From what I've been able to find out, Harlin, you're not doing too well yourself. You've been out of work for nearly four years due to health reasons. According to the resources that I have, you're suffering from chronic depression, as most of us are. As well as the pain and injuries that come with having that disease for so long. You're bouncing from shelter to shelter until they tell you to leave. Through no fault of your own, but they don't want to have long-term people there." Harlin wanted to hang up, but the next thing he said intrigued him. "Caleb is in a position to help you, and he really wants to do whatever you need to make your life better in any way possible. You need only come here and meet with all of us then, while I'm not sure what you want to do after that. I do know that none of us have a hold over you. You're free to come and go as you please."

Harlin thought about what the man was saying. He knew of them. All of the babies born from Berkley. Mostly it was the women and how he had stalked them for weeks before taking them into what he'd called his lair. Only a barn where he would… he would hurt them. His own mom had begged him not to leave her every time he took a woman to rape. Mom wanted to make her place his so that he'd come back to her. Their relationship, even before he left home, was only violence and screaming at each other. But that was the way his mother had wanted it. To be—

"Harlin, are you all right? Are you still there?" He told Joey that he was thinking about shit that he and the others might like to know. "I know that we would. As I said, all of us have lost our mothers. I'm sure that whatever you can give us will be something profoundly helpful. Just to have an understanding of Howard will help us deal with the pain that he caused not just our mothers but us as well."

"I don't think you're going to say that when you read my mom's diary, or I guess I should say diaries. She still writes in one at the place she's at. They hand them off to me once or twice a year. Also, you should know that I'm no better off with my mother than the others are without theirs. She was sick before I came along, and Berkley fed into her way of life with her being dependent on others that would try and help her as well as bi-polar." Joey said he was sorry, and it felt sincere, too, like he meant it. "Berkley lived with us, as I said. He would drift out of our lives for a while and then come back. My mother thought that he was a god of some sort. I don't know how long he was a part of her life before I noticed him coming around a lot more than the others. Then it was just him. When it was clear that I wasn't going to be lying for him or her again to bill collectors or social services, I got tossed aside. Literally, but I do have her books. And you're welcome to read over them as much as you wish. As I said, I don't think you're going to like what you find. I know that I don't like it when I get a new one from her. I want you to know too that I don't know how much of it's true. As I said, my mom has been in some kind of mental crisis since before I was born." He paused for a few seconds before plunging on. "In the first few books, it has how the two of the stalked your mothers. How my mom would follow yours around until he got a pattern, all worked out on when to take them. How to take them, as well as if he'd need rope or tape. It's all in there. I don't believe that she had anything to do with the actual rape, but she is just as guilty as he is for what happened." He waited for Joey to tell him that he'd changed his mind and that there was no way that he was going to be a part of their big happy family. It only just occurred to him that Harlin really did want to be with them. If nothing more than to be able to be around people like himself. To be a part of something good in his life. So when Joey spoke, Harlin was braced for the blow.

"I'm so sorry for what you had to endure, Harlin. My heart aches for you knowing what sort of person he was and that you had to go through that. And your mom. If you ask me, you would have been better off without her around than to have her. And for that, I'm profoundly sorry." Harlin felt the tears fill his eyes. As Joey continued, he had to lean back against the wall in the kitchen so that he'd not fall to the floor. It was the first time in his life that it seemed to him that someone sincerely understood his life. "I'm going to talk to Caleb and see how long it will take us to get to you. Don't be surprised if you're greeted at the door with a bunch of new family for you." That shocked him to his very core.

"Did you hear what I said to you? That I knew about what was going on through the books? That I have hard evidence of what each of your mothers went through? Are you listening to me?" He said that he'd heard. But he also knew that he more than likely suffered more than any of the rest of them had. "Oh, Joey, you've no idea. None. You can't even imagine the suffering that I went through once Howard stayed with my mom."

Harlin was thirty-nine years old, and he was sitting on the floor of his kitchen, sobbing and holding a towel to his face like he'd done as a child. It had been his only way to not get beaten harder by not allowing his *parents* to hear him. The towel was much like he'd had in his blanket he'd had. A sense of security, no matter how insufficient it seemed now. They were both something — the towel and the blanket—that he'd use later to tend to his wounds when he was alone.

Babbling now, telling Joey all the little things that he could remember. How his mother would hold him down so that Howard could beat him. How to this day, he couldn't feel emotions like other people. Nor could he, Harlin thought, allow people to get close to him for fear that they'd emotionally destroy him. Moreso than he was already. He could hear the sadness in Joey's voice. And when he blew his nose, that told him that he'd been crying as well. Harlin had no idea why but it made him feel closer to the other man.

"When Caleb and Tabby found me, I was holding a gun in my hand to end my life." He could hear the pain in the other man's voice, and it made him think that he was a kindred spirit. "Tabby, she's a wonderful person, and Caleb's wife took the gun from me and put it to my forehead and told me that she'd end my life for me if that was what I wanted. Telling me that it wouldn't bother her to do it as her prints would be on nothing. She told me later that it hurt her to her soul to have said that to me. And every single minute of every day, I find that I love that woman for what she did more than anyone.

And I, because of her, have a wife and five of the best children ever. Please say that you'll come here with us? Please? We'll leave within the hour to be there."

After giving him his address and a good number in which to reach him, the two of them spoke for another half hour. When he hung up with Joey, Harlin sat there on the floor, sobbing like a small child. Something he'd not done in a good long time was having a good cry for himself. And he'd done it twice today.

The place that he was staying in was in a place of flux for him. It had been his mother's place when he'd been in the military. Even before that, when he'd been a child. And now that she was in a state-funded home, they wanted the money for it so that it would cover the costs of her stay. The very one that she'd shared with Howard when he'd been alive, as a matter of fact.

Boxing up the crap, because that's all most of it was, had been easy for him. Nothing here held any good memories. There were no mementos from when he'd been in military school that she saved. Not even his old room was anything that he thought about saving something from. It was just crap she'd accumulated when she'd been able to live here.

Harlin hadn't been back here for any reason since he'd been a boy of six when he'd been sent away to school. There were no memories here that he wanted to waste his time on thinking about again. So he was tossing everything that he pulled out of cabinets and drawers.

Howard had been killed a while ago, but it looked as if his mom had been waiting for him to come home like before. There was still some of his clothing in her closet. Shoes lined up at the door for him to use. There were even a few Christmas wrapped gifts with his name on them that she'd continued to purchase.

Even in the pantry, things were marked with his name on them. Harlin remembered not being allowed to touch any of his food, for he'd bought it for himself. Which had been a lie. Mother had bought everything for the two of them.

Packing what little he'd come here with, he was glad now that he'd washed up his clothing last night and had dried them earlier today. That was about all he ever had was clothing, toiletries, some dried fruit and bottles of water. He even still used the same duffle that he'd had in the service with markings on it from all the different places he'd been to while serving his country. Not that he had any money to replace anything that he could use, but Harlin wasn't sure that he'd even do that. It worked, and it was his. That was enough reason for him to keep using his things.

Making the call for the donation service to come and get the things he'd promised them, Harlin helped them load all the furniture into their vans. A bed frame, some living room things, as well as a plethora of lamps with shades of so many shapes and sizes that he wondered where she might have gotten them. A couple of the men that had come had stayed to help him wrap the mattresses and box springs in plastic to be put out with the trash. He'd not even knew there was a rule about that.

The food had all been expired by the time he'd gotten around to coming here, and that too went out to the trash. By the time he and the realtor were going through the empty house, Harlin was about as emotionally exhausted as he'd ever been. He didn't think that there were going to be a lot of people beating down the door to buy the place, but he didn't care. It would be, thankfully, one less thing that he'd have to worry about.

Harlin turned toward the street when he heard

someone calling his name. He didn't have time to react nor see who was calling for him when he was suddenly being hugged. Being engulfed in strong arms nearly took him to the ground again what, with his heart still on a rollercoaster of emotions.

Holding onto the man as he said he had him over and over, Harlin had an overwhelming need to never let him go. He was weak in the knees. His eyes were filled with emotional tears. When he did let the man go, Harlin was embraced by two more men while the first man, Caleb, he told him, introduced him to everyone that had come with him.

"My name is Caleb Anderson. You know Joey Phillips. This is his wife, Yazzie. They left their children with the nanny." He was gripped hard by her as well as Joey and loved every second of it. "This is Martin Hamilton and his wife, Gracie. Like you, Martin is our brother. That beautiful lady to their right is Tabby, my wife. She keeps all of us in line."

They all hugged him several times, and there were a lot of tears shed. Not a tissue in the house, but he had plenty of toilet paper to go around. He took them into the house with him and was sorry that he couldn't at least offer them a glass of water as everything had been taken away. None of them were upset by his lack of planning, it seemed. It was Joey who asked if this had been his family home.

"I guess you could call it that. My mom lived here with Howard right up until he was killed. I was sent away when I was barely old enough to tie my shoes, but I think that might have worked out better." They all told him how sorry they were for that. "I've put the house on the market, but there won't be any proceeds from it. The nursing home that my mother will be staying in for the rest of her days will take all of it. I'm sure that had there been anything else, they would have taken that as well. But sadly, she only had this home to use. She's getting the care that she deserves, as much as I hate to sound like that. And after I finish this up, I'm not going to be around for her anymore. Not that I was for some time now, but that's all water under the bridge, as the saying goes."

"Do you have another place to stay? I've made our reservations at the hotel here in town for you as well while we visit a little." Harlin told Caleb that he'd not thought beyond getting this mess taken care of. "I can understand that. Not that my mom left me a mess, but it was nice to be able to get out of our home and into something else. Too many memories. I'm not saying yours are anything like mine were, but memories are still difficult to deal with all the time."

"Yes, but as you said, yours weren't nearly as bad as mine are." Caleb told him he was sorry. "No. I'm the one that should be sorry. I'm a little on the tender side today when I think of my childhood. I shouldn't take it out on you guys. Not until I get to know you better, at least."

Everyone laughed, and it was a sound that he thought he could get used to. However, as he was standing there, listening to others about their trip here, Tabby pulled his arm to her and lifted up his sleeve to look at the scars there. Then she did the same thing to his other wrist. They were long and narrow. There was no hiding the fact as to why they were there. He'd slit his wrists. Twice as a matter of course.

"Don't do this again, please?" He just stared at her. "You're my brother as much as the others are, and it would break my heart to know that you didn't come to me or one of the others when you needed us. We'll all be here for you too, Harlin. Forever if that is what you need from us."

"I've had a very difficult life, Tabby. I've seen and done things that would turn your hair white and age you considerably if you knew what they were." She hugged him, put both her arms around him and held him tightly. "Tabby, you're going to make this big Marine cry if you keep being nice to me, and that's not anything to be proud of."

"I'll never tell." That little three word sentence had him fighting harder than he'd had as a child to not let anyone see him cry. It meant so much to him that it had become too much. Harlin leaned down to her and sobbed on her shoulder. Holding her as tightly as she was him.

"I've never been this emotional before." She said because he'd never been allowed to be emotional before. "Christ, Tabby, you're going to make me a weak-assed man if I hang out with you and the others too much."

"Then stay with us forever, and I'll fight your battles for you when you need it. Any one of us will." He nodded, unable to speak around the lump in his throat and the melting of his frozen heart. She pulled back and looked up at him. "Come on now. You get cleaned up, and we'll put your things in the limo. We'll have a lovely dinner, and then you'll come back home with us and meet your nieces and nephews. They're a hoot, and you'll love them too."

Before he knew it, Harlin was in the back of a limo with the other six. After Caleb had a long conversation with the realtor, Harlin found himself sitting in a nice restaurant with his family. Family. It was a word that, while he'd never had a good one, the word had a really nice ring to it, and he might like to get used to having them around.

"I've bought the house for the amount you were asking, Harlin. Next week, if you'd not mind, I'm going to have it torn down and one put in its place. It'll be a rental that will be taken care of by my attorneys, and the money will go to the care of your mother. She might be a horrible person, but she's your mom, and that's the way she'll be taken care of." Harlin thanked him. "You're very welcome. We're family now, and family takes care of each other."

When the waiter brought out their food, Harlin couldn't help but smile. The dishes were so beautiful. It was like looking at a masterpiece. The smells of the food made his mouth water and his stomach grumble in anticipation. Everyone around the table was talking and laughing, and he felt himself relax as he watched them enjoy each other's company.

The conversation was lively and filled with stories about their lives that would make most people laugh or cry. But for Harlin, it was different—it felt like a glimpse into what life could be like if he stayed with them forever. He found himself drawn to every word they said, wanting to know more about each one of their lives.

As dinner progressed, Harlin couldn't help but feel grateful for this chance to be part of something special—a family that accepted him despite his broken past and gave him hope for the future. After dessert had been served and they were getting ready to leave, Harlin finally opened up to them about what all he'd been through after all these years.

When he finished speaking, there were tears in everyone's eyes, including his own. They all hugged him tightly and promised that no matter what happened in the future, they would always be there for him—just as Tabby had said earlier that day, forever, if that was what he needed from them. Harlin knew then that no matter where life took him next, he'd never forget this night spent with his newfound family at the restaurant; it would stay with him always as an important reminder of how far he'd come on this journey toward happiness.

~*~

Raven stood up when her client, Mrs. Glenna Pastor,

was called so the judge could hear her side of the trouble her children were causing her. Stating Mrs. Pastor's name and Raven's affiliation with her, the judge asked her what was going on.

"Mrs. Pastor has been in a nursing home for the last ten years, your honor. The state takes her social security checks each month as payment as well as her pension from working for the state as a road crew when she was stronger. She worked for another ten years after she should have been able to retire just to have money for her bills. Her children, the four of them, are now requesting that she come live with them throughout the year, each of them taking her for three months at a time. As specified in the contract with the nursing home, if Mrs. Pastor is too much for the children, they'll no longer be able to return her to the nursing home. Ever. Also, if they were to take her back, even if it was for only a few days, the paperwork would need to be redone to get her back in the state-funded program to take care of her needs." Judge Sheppard asked what the issue was. "Mrs. Pastor doesn't want to live with them. They treated her poorly when she was living with them before she was able to get into the nursing home. This is the fifth time that they've decided that they want her to come and live with them. Each time, she gets poor care from them and usually ends up in the hospital with bed sores as well as dehydration and malnutrition. According to Mrs. Pastor, they would lock her in her room all day and night and only check on her to see if she was still alive or not. She doesn't want to go through that again, your honor. It was bad enough that she wasn't getting proper medical care, but they would take the money that was to be used for her and spend it on things that they wanted. Nothing, you'll note on what they needed."

"And you have proof of this?" Asking to come to the dais, she handed the paperwork from the last five home trials for the family to the judge. Not only did she have the proper paperwork from her doctors, but also all hospital stays that had anything to do with her poor health when it was needed. "It says here that her meds were never picked up on time and that according to her advocate, you, I'm assuming, they were sold off instead of given to her."

"They'd not care a fig newton if I was starving or not, sir." Mrs. Pastor, for being in her late eighties, was as sharp as a tack. Also, she didn't suffer fools all that well. That's why Raven had requested to be her guardian, and that was what most of this trial was going to be for. Hopefully. To keep her family from doing this to her every several months when they'd need a few bucks to use. "Why, that oldest one of mine—I'm ashamed to admit this to anyone—but he'd punish me like I'm a child by taking my food from me when I didn't make it to the bathroom on time. Ungrateful bastards. The lot of them. How was I to make it to the bathroom when it's nowhere close to my room, and they have big locks on the doors, I ask you. And big old locks, too, that weren't on my side so that I could undo them. Padlocks, if you can believe it. Padlocks. I tell you, they're ungrateful. The only person in the world that treats me with any kind of dignity is this young woman right here. She's been my rock since this nightmare began. Those kids of mine need to spend time with themselves and not be trying to take all my money for their own pleasures. Why, when I was living with my daughter, she bought her a new car and wouldn't even take me to the doctors in it for fear of me wetting myself in it. I might be old, but I do know when I have to potty, for crip's sake. Better than them kids of hers know, I'm thinking. Then when she decided that she'd gotten all she could from me, she tossed me in a nursing home and lost her car on account of the home taking the money for my care." Mrs. Pastor laughed. "Got her car repossessed, too, on account of her not getting my checks anymore. That's all they care about. Getting my pension and social security checks to spend on crapola they don't need. Darned kids. If I had to do it over, I'd of not bothered with them. Ungrateful... well, I already said that, but I think it bears repeating. They're ungrateful."

The judge was trying hard not to laugh. If he knew anything about the elderly woman, he'd be careful about laughing at her. While she used a wheelchair to get around, she could get around better than most people in their sixties. It was just so that when she got tired like she did less times than Raven did, then she'd have a place to plop down. Her words, not Raven's.

"Ms. Tanner, you've been taking care of Mrs. Pastor for how long now?" She told him about the last ten years. "And you're an attorney for her as well, I can see here."

"Yes, sir. I was working for a firm when her case came across my desk. I'd already decided that being an attorney wasn't what I wanted in life and had given my two weeks. Mr. Palmer of Palmer and Palmer, told me that if I took care that Mrs. Pastor was well represented, he'd pay me my usual salary so long as I worked for her through them. I took the job after one visit with Mrs. Pastor, meeting her family at the same time. As Glenna is so fond of saying, it was a show of shows, and there wasn't even a good meal to go with it." He asked her if she was still an attorney. "I am your honor. I keep my license up so that if something comes up, I will be prepared to care for all her needs."

"Mrs. Pastor, other than your pension and Social Security, is there any other money that could be had from your estate?" She told him that she had insurance out the wahoo. Again, the judge laughed but coughed to cover it when she glared at him. "I'm assuming you have a will made out as to what happens to your wahoo money?"

"Yes, sir. Missy Raven here wouldn't do that for me. She said that if I wanted to do anything with that, I should get me an estate attorney so that no one could say that whatever was in it that she'd not had a thing to do with it. So those ungrateful kids of mine couldn't say that she'd done it to profit herself or something along those lines. Wouldn't even let me tell her what it was going to say nor who the attorney was." The judge said that was brilliant of her. "Well, she is a brilliant girl. No cobwebs between her ears, that's for sure."

"Mrs. Pastor, you are a pleasure to speak to today. If you and Ms. Tanner could wait here while I—" The back doors to the courtroom were opened with a loud bang. Every person in the room that was armed put their hands on their weapons. Even her. "What is the meaning of this intrusion? Who are you? And what are you doing interrupting a court proceeding?"

The six people that came into the courtroom were none other than the four children of Mrs. Pastor as well as two spouses. Raven didn't know who the wives belonged to, but she was willing to bet that it made very little difference at the moment. After explaining to the judge who they were and a general name for the bunch of them, the six of them continued to argue about who got to sit at the front table to get this 'shit over with' so they could start getting paid. She knew that William always thought that he should be the first in line for whatever was going on. Dumbass.

The gavel banged on the dais several times before the idiots looked anywhere near being finished arguing. It wasn't until Mrs. Pastor put her fingers into her mouth and let out a shrill whistle that they abruptly shut up. Raven was prepared for it as she'd heard her do it before, but the judge and the others in the courtroom were shocked to silence. Everyone but Glenna's children.

"Sit down and shut up before I have the lot of you arrested for being born." The oldest, William, said she wasn't able to do anything and she'd best be keeping her mouth shut. "You come on over here, William Hunter Pastor and I'll show you what I can do and not do. You were told to be here at nine. It's nearly noon. Why can't you take instructions well enough to be on time to go someplace? You were even late when being born. I should have taken that as a sign about you. Are you more addled than I thought you might be?"

"Why do they need to make things so early in the morning for anyway? I was sleeping. Then April Showers comes along and jerks me out of my nice bed like she's got some right to be doing that. Mom, you didn't raise her right. She's a stupid jerk-face." William Hunter, his mother called all her children by their first and middle names, so the kids referred to themselves that way as well glared at her. "What is she doing here anyway? I thought that this was just going to be you and us getting you home with us. Don't you want that, Momma? To come and live with your children instead of sitting around on your duff all day with none of us around? Even the grandkids are looking forward to you being around for them to babysit."

"Actually, no, I don't want to live with any of you. Having you around when you were little was bad enough. I like it just where I am. As for me being around your kids? Well, they're as bad as the four of you are. Always with their hands out, thinking I'm going to fill it for them. I'm not, just so you know. You either." William Hunter asked his momma if Raven had put her up to saying that. "You know, I do have a brain, you dummy. I can and do speak for myself. She's here because she doesn't have to be borrowing brain cells to know what time to be somewhere when you've been told a dozen times when it starts. Not to mention, I don't have to be continually paying her money just so she'll do things for me when I need them. Now sit your bottoms down and don't make me have to come over there. I will beat your bottoms; you see that I won't. I should have done it more when you were little, and I'd have me a better set of children. But I put that blame squarely on the head of your father. Spoiled you. He did. Thinking you're grander than you really are. Now hush before I have one of you go out and pick me a switch off that tree out front so I can beat some—though I'm thinking that it won't matter a hill of beans—Beating some sense into your heads would just go in one area and plum right out of your ears."

The judge left the room at some point, but the bailiff stood by the other Prestons while in the courtroom. Every time one of them started to get loud, he'd tell them to shut up, never taking his hand off his weapon. Raven and Mrs. Pastor spoke quietly at the other table.

"If he comes back with you having to go to your family's home, I'm going to apply for being your guardian like we discussed." Mrs. Pastor told her that she should just apply for it anyway, as her idiots weren't going to be giving up. "I don't want to rock the boat any more than we have to. Some of the paperwork the judge has is about me doing that for you. We'll just have to wait and see, I guess. At least he's not thrown us out of here because of your kids. That's a good sign."

"I guess." She looked over at her children, so Raven did the same. They were arguing again about who was going to take their mommy first. "They're fools. I hope someone sees that before they kill me off. They will too. If I die on my own, they're not going to be happy about nothing ever again. And they'll come after you on account of you being my friend."

"I'm not worried about them, Mrs. Pastor. You just worry about what kind of things you're going to do to your room when you get back to the nursing home. I'm glad they found you a room bigger apartment than the one you have now and are willing to hold it for you. It'll be nice for you to be able to have a sewing room again, I'm thinking." She said that was exciting her the most. "Good. Once this is all settled, hopefully in your favor, you can go on sewing and enjoying life to the fullest. You and I will still have our weekly shopping and lunch, and your children will just be a fart in the wind as you're so fond of calling them."

"I should have kicked them in the head more. Might have made something click in that empty space they have up there. I doubt it, but I might well have enjoyed it a little. Too much, I would imagine." She looked over her shoulder to her children before smiling again. "That Betsy Sue, she's put on a few pounds since her divorce. She keeps eating like she is, and she'll be in a nursing home too. They'll have to put her on one of those diet plans before too much longer. Darned kids."

Glenna, as she insisted Raven call her, didn't care at all for her offspring. She was forever telling her that she'd not wanted her husband, much less any kids of his, when they married. But since he'd asked her daddy before asking her, she didn't get the opportunity to turn him down. And she would have too. He had been a good deal older than her and meaner than a rattlesnake, to boot.

Her father had her married off to Mr. Gleason Pastor before she had her wedding dress picked out. Something that she regretted more than marrying Gleason was not having a pretty wedding like all her cousins did. But done was done, another saying from Glenna, and she found herself using it more often than not.

Raven wasn't stupid. Not by a long shot. She was actually very brilliant. After graduating at the top of her class from Harvard, she not only had a doctorate in law, but she also had a degree in social humanities. That was why she was able to take care of Glenna herself and not have someone doing it for the elderly woman. There was also the fact that she dearly loved the elderly woman. She was like a grandma that she never had.

Glenna and Mr. Pastor had a rather tumultuous marriage, mostly due to his temper and his domineering ways. The more she tried to stand up for herself, the worse he got. He would go off on long trips for weeks at a time, and when he returned, it was like living with a ticking time bomb. You never knew if or when it was going to go off, but you were always ready for the explosion that could come at any moment.

And yet, despite all of this, Glenna still managed to keep her head up high and take care of her husband's needs as best as she could. She looked after him when he was sick and took care of his every need, no matter how small or insignificant they may have been.

Glenna also taught Raven many valuable lessons about life during their weekly shopping trips together, such as not letting anyone dictate your happiness, treating others with respect regardless of their situation in life, and being grateful for what you have, even if it is less than perfect. Every day that Raven spent with Glenna was an invaluable lesson in compassion and love that she will cherish forever.

After an hour, the judge sent someone out to say they'd rejoin the courtroom at two. They were told to go and get some lunch, and he'd have his verdict when they all returned. While she and Glenna were leaving the courtroom, William was asking when they got to say anything. Raven didn't hear the answer, figuring that they'd get their say when they returned. Or not. They'd already pissed a lot of people off today.

They settled at the dairy bar across the street from the courthouse. It was really busy, and they opted to sit under the large willow tree that had several tables and chairs around it. It wasn't just a peaceful place, but it was quite in the little town too. After getting their food and drinks, Raven looked around the small town that she'd gown up in and wondered at all the new additions. She was particularly happy with the greenhouse renovations.

Glenna noticed Raven's gaze and chuckled. "You're like a tourist in your own hometown. Everything looks different, doesn't it?"

Raven smiled. "Yeah, it does. But it's nice to see that they're making improvements to the town. It's still as charming as ever."

Glenna nodded. "Charming, yes. But I've seen this town go through some tough times. When the mill shut down, it hit everyone hard. But we bounced back. We always do."

Raven listened to Glenna's stories about the town's history and the people who lived there. She loved hearing about the resilience of the community and how they came together during difficult times. It made her appreciate the town even more.

As they finished their lunch, William and his siblings walked into the dairy bar. Raven tensed up, but Glenna just gave them a sly smile. "Well, well, look who it is. My little farts in the wind."

William scowled. "How can you talk about us like that, Momma? We're your children."

Glenna shrugged. "You may be my children, but you're not acting like it. You're here trying to take away what's rightfully mine."

"It's not rightfully yours, Mom. Dad left everything to us."

Glenna snorted. "Your father didn't leave anything to me when he was alive, and I sure as hell don't need anything from him now that he's dead. You all just want his money. You don't care about me or what I want."

William Hunter rolled his eyes and huffed. "You just wait until I get you in my home again. Then we'll see what we get or don't get."

Donald James approached the table and crossed his arms over his chest, eyeing her lunch plate. "Momma, you're going to buy us some lunch. Don't you be giving me shit about it, either. We had come here and didn't get to have anything before this was called on us. Besides, we all left the house without our wallets. Just give me what you have on you, and we'll make due." Glenna told her son, Donald James, that she didn't have her wallet either and that Raven had bought her lunch for her. "Then she'll buy for us too. Give me your credit card, girly, and I'll think about returning it to you. You've caused us a lot of trouble. I hope you know that. Why in the hell would you have them start this thing at the crack of dawn anyway? You trying to make us pissed off?"

"Really? Not that it matters to me one lick, but I'm not giving you my credit card, nor am I going to purchase you any lunch. The crack of dawn occurred about eight hours ago, you idiot, and I didn't set the time. The courthouse did. Deal with it." He asked her why she wasn't buying them lunch like she had his momma. "I don't like you. None of you, as a matter of fact. So if you did indeed forget your wallets, which I don't believe for a second, then ask your wife. I can see that she has a nice handbag that looks stuffed with something. I'm not going to feed you shit. Get away from here before I call the cops on you."

"You got no reason to call anyone on us, Blackbird. You have a stupid name, too, by the way." A man wearing a suit and tie came and sat with her and Glenna. While she had no idea who he was, it looked to her like Donald did. "You already called them on us? Why? We haven't done a thing wrong to you yet."

"I know that, but it's the 'yet' that bothers me the most. Go away, Donald, before I have you arrested for being a dumbass." The man stood up, but he didn't say a word as he stared at Donald. Raven could see the gun at his side as well as the one that was just under the hem of his suit coat. "Donald, I wouldn't mess with this man if I were you. He's smart enough to shoot first and not ever ask questions of you later. Go away before I have to sell tickets to let people see you get your ass handed to you. Again."

Donald walked away, mumbling under his breath about how he was being mistreated again and again. When the man was brought his food, Glenna asked him who he was. The smile on the man was contagious, and she smiled back at him.

"I'm Joey Phillips. My wife and I were out walking with the kids after their orientation at the school over there when she heard the arguing about lunch. She's going to be joining us soon." Glenna asked if he was a cop. "I work for the government when they need me, but yes, mostly, I work for the local police department. May I ask what is going on with the Pastor kids?"

Glenna explained how sorry she was about them being her children. She also gave Joey the run down on what was going on with them. A lovely woman and five of the most beautiful children sat down with them. The kids were each carrying a boxed-up lunch, even the smallest little boy, and one of the staff brought out one for the mother.

It surprised her to figure out that the woman was blind. Joey introduced her to them by telling her where they were seated. He also told them the names and ages of their children. Then he explained, as most would forget about, where her food was located on her plate by using clock numbers. It thrilled Raven to no end to hear someone talking to another person in such a kind tone. Unlike the Pastor children did to their own mother. Raven asked about her blindness.

Raven couldn't help but feel a sense of empathy toward the blind woman. She knew what it was like to have someone control her life and make her feel trapped. She took a bite of her hotdog and savored the taste. It had been a while since she had a meal like this, surrounded by such good company.

"I've been blind since childhood. Sometimes I can fool most people into believing I'm sighted, but when we're out in public, so I don't wear most of what I'm eating, I like to know where things are on my plate." The kids were so polite in helping the youngest child, George, to get a cup of ketchup on his plate to dip his dog in. She did the same thing. Ketchup was a food group to her. "They're all ready for school this fall, and we came out to celebrate."

"I loved school when I was younger." She wiped mustard off of Madison's face when she bit into her hotdog too. "I've been meaning to go back to study something else for a while now. But Mrs. Pastor has been keeping me on my toes. Not that I mind a bit. She keeps me sane, I think."

"Oh, go on with you. You know that we're having fun." Raven laughed and said that they were having fun even when they probably shouldn't be.

"If I can stay put, I'm going to be a good deal happier than I am right now. I no more want to live with my kids than I want to have someone plucking my fingernails out and making an art project with them. No siree, baby. I don't want that."

They talked until it was time for them to go back into the courtroom. Joey joined them inside, telling them that he'd feel better if they had more representation than they did now. She was actually glad for the extra pair of eyes. Whatever the judge said, it wasn't going to be a good thing for anyone, no matter how it went. But she would hope for things to go Glenna's way. She deserved it more than anyone else.

Chapter 2

Joey watched the people in the courtroom. Mostly the two women in front of him at the table reserved for them. He had no doubt that it would come out in favor of the two women. If for no other reason than they'd not pissed off the judge since he'd been in here with them. While he did know their relationship, that of attorney to client, he also knew that it was a great deal more than that. The two of them acted like they were grandma to granddaughter. Then he looked at the six people sitting at the other table. They were related by blood, and he didn't doubt that soon, they'd be shedding a bit of it too.

Chairs had been brought in so they could all sit around the same table. Not that it stopped the bickering, but he was sure that the judge was handling that well enough. He'd tell them to shut up, and they'd do it for a few minutes, then start back up. Usually louder and meaner than before. Mostly it was the two sons telling their momma from across the room that she did indeed want to live with them and that the kids, theirs, he assumed, would love seeing them. Glenna just stared at them until they shut up or turned away for the same few minutes. When the judge cleared his throat for the third time, everyone quieted down and looked at him.

"Ms. Tanner, I've been able to go over the information that you've gathered for me. This is better than I get for some murder trials, I have to admit. But it's everything that I need for me to make a decision today." Judge Martin glared at the kids' table and looked as if he was daring them to speak. "Now. Without further ado, in the case of Pastor versus Pastor in all, I'm giving Raven Tanner full guardianship of Glenna Pastor. I'm also declaring Glenna Pastor of sound mind and able to make any decisions that she needs in order to make this trial happen. Also, before I forget, her will. It's been filed, and just so there is no wrongdoing anymore, I've requested a notarized copy of it for myself. Her attorney for that said that he'd had Mrs. Pastor tested at the time, and she passed with flying colors. Stating that she is of sound mind when that occurred as well. Ms. Tanner will take care of Mrs. Pastor's legal needs when they arise, as well as make sure that her bills are paid each month in full if asked to do so. Ms. Tanner will do so until such time that she either feels Mrs. Pastor can do this on her own — which I do not recommend — or she passes away. You understand what I'm saying, Mrs. Pastor, don't you?"

"I do, sir. I do. Raven is going to make sure that I'm well cared for, as she's been doing for a while now, as well as not taking any of my money. She'll also keep the buzzards away —" She looked over at her children, and Joey had to laugh — "when I'm dead and gone. Thank you, your honor. You did me right on this, and I can't thank you enough." William Hunter stood up and looked around the courtroom, and Joey could see on his face that he was more confused looking than ever.

"So what happens to us? I mean, how are we going to get her money? That woman over there, she's forever telling us no, we can't get into our own momma's account anymore. That is our momma, not hers, and we do need for her to help us out on occasion. We can't even stay at her home no more to hide out when we need to." The judge asked William

Hunter how old he was. "Near fifty. I think." He looked at his wife, and she nodded, then shrugged. "I don't know what that has to do with what I've asked you, sir. Our daddy paid into her getting that social check, and we should at least get a part of it. Momma's job was raising us kids up the way that Daddy wanted her to. Now she's doing things her way, and well, judge, we don't care for it. It's not fair for her to be making her own decisions like she's in charge. As for her pension? Well, as the oldest, I should be able to have that because what is she going to do with it sitting around on her butt all day at that home. Did you know that my momma eats better than we do whilst she's staying there? That's not fair. Not one bit."

"Fair or not, I've made my decision. And I'd think that a man your age would be able to know that he has his shoes on the wrong feet when out, as well as bringing his wallet to town. What if I were to have you pulled over on the way home? You driving without a license is against the law. Or do you not care about that sort of thing." He told him that the police took his license about four years ago when he'd been struck three times. "I haven't any idea what that might mean. But I'm assuming, and probably wrong, that you've been pulled over three times? For what? Speeding or drinking? Or both, perhaps?"

"I don't drink. My daddy told us all that to drink shows how stupid you are. And if you were caught at it while driving, the police should bang your head against the car until you're smart enough to remember is what he'd told us." Joey had to cover his mouth when a burble of laughter came out when the judge asked him if he thought that was the only cause of his being stupid. "I don't know what you mean about that, sir, I don't, but what about my momma's money? It's only a little bit. She can get herself a job doing dishes or something to make it work for her."

"And what sort of job do you do, Mr. Pastor? Perhaps it wouldn't hurt any of you to get a job so that your momma can keep what she's worked hard for all her life." William Hunter seemed to be shocked that the judge would suggest such a thing. "It's just a thought, but I'm wondering how you afford to buy your momma gifts at Christmas or Mother's Day?"

"We're her kids, not the other way around." Judge Martin asked him what he meant by that. "She's the one that should be buying us gifts, not us her. Daddy always saw to it that she used her own money when it was our birthdays and such. Daddy used his money for paying the bills and —"

"Your 'daddy' didn't work a day in his life, you idiots. And I purchased your gifts because I thought that I should. Then after one of you little shits told me that I should have spent more on you heathens than I had, I didn't buy them anymore. The house, the land and the food on your table were mine. When my own father passed away, regretting every day that he'd made me marry your father, he left everything to me." William asked how much of that was left over. "Not a penny as far as you're concerned. You'll not get anything from my estate, nor will you ever set a foot in that house again either. You all need to be getting out of there before I have you arrested for just being my children. Anyone that has spent more than ten minutes with you would understand and put you in a cell and throw away the keys. Damned fools. Get a job, the lot of you and pay your own bills."

Joey stood up when William and Donald looked as if they were coming after their mother. Both of them backed down, but that didn't stop them from hurling threats at her. As soon as the judge said that the hearing was final, that his decision stood,

Joey escorted the two women out into the waiting limo that Caleb had sent for them.

Glenna laughed. She laughed so hard that he worried for her for a little while. Then she looked at Raven and hugged her tightly. He'd been wrong about their relationship. It wasn't like family at all but better. Best of friends, that's what the two of them were.

"Oh, we need to celebrate." Joey was all for that but also wanted to get home to his family. Before he could decline the offer, Raven said that she had to talk to her bosses about the win and to go home and take a nap. "Yes, I think you might be right on that. But I get to go to the nursing home again. With a bigger room and I'll have my sewing things brought to me out of storage. Oh, I'm so excited about all this."

The bump to the car knocked the elderly lady off her seat. As Raven was trying to get herself upright along with the elderly lady, they were knocked from behind again. Turning to look out the back window that was shattered, he could see the Pastor family, all six of them crammed into a small SUV, laughing and running up on them again. Joey told the driver to make a turn, hard and fast.

As the family drove by them, he pulled out his

phone and called Caleb. "You're not going to believe this, but we've been hit by the family I was telling you about." He gave him all the details that he had, including the license plate of the car that was coming at them from the front now. "Your driver is doing all he can to keep us from being killed, but we're going to need for you to meet us at the hospital. No one is really hurt, but we need — Christ."

The other car plowed into the side of the limo. He was so glad to see Raven pull Glenna off the seat and onto the floorboard to keep her from being covered in glass. Raven was cut up, but he couldn't tell how badly right now. When the little car backed up and hit them a second time, he heard the airbags go off in the front, and then he was out.

Waking in the hospital, he was glad to see that Caleb was with him. Tabby wasn't, so he thought she'd been with the other women. At least he hoped someone was with them. When Glenna joined him in the private room off the emergency department, he was sorry to see that her arm was in a cast and the wheelchair that he'd put into the trunk before leaving had sustained substantial cosmetic damage. Glenna told him that it was replaceable, but he wasn't.

"Thank you for that. Is Raven all right? I saw

at one point that she was bleeding, but then we were hit again, and I blacked out." He tried to sit up, but Caleb told him to lie still. "I don't know why I'm here. Can you explain what is going on?" His head started to scream at him. "But use small words and a quiet voice." Caleb laughed.

"As you know, you were hit from behind by the Pastor family. Twice, the police believe. Then when you dodged them the third time, they came out of the alley down from where you were and plodded the car in the side. After that, they kept hitting the car with theirs until their car just stopped moving. They're all down the hall, blaming Glenna and Raven for their *accident*. It wasn't an accident. The police are calling it attempted murder. They're saying they didn't plan on hitting you guys. I guess they meant they'd not meant to hit you about a dozen times. The police are with them, so you don't have to worry about them coming in here for another go at you guys." He asked about Raven again. It was Glenna that answered this time.

"She's in surgery. Took a hard knock to her head like you did when she hit the back window. Also, she has some broken ribs, her leg is busted in two places, and she has a cut on her other leg when the car was turned upside down from the hits. They're fixing her leg up so that she'll be able to walk when it's all healed up." Glenna was crying by then, and it hurt him that the elderly lady had been injured too. "She's a better daughter than I ever had, and now she's going to be hurting because of my idiot children. I don't know what I'm going to do without her. I just don't. At least I have me a nursing home to care for me. She's got nobody but herself to make sure that she does what she's supposed to. I don't know if you might not have noticed this or not, but she's a stubborn little thing."

Caleb assured her that he'd make sure that Raven had the best of care and that before he'd allow her to go home on her own, he'd make sure that she was safe and sound too. He even said she could live with him and Tabby once she was released.

"I'd let her come and live with us, but I think being around my five kids will be hard on her. Sometimes it is on me too." He laughed when Glenna thanked them both for making her laugh. "So, can someone tell me when I get to go home?" Caleb smiled at him before speaking again.

"Tabby and Yazzie are down the hall getting as much information as they can about the Pastors while the police are talking to them. Neither of them can be seen through the two-way mirror, so that's good for us. As I said, they're blaming it on Raven. Who I like, by the way, just for what she did to keep Glenna safe. For now, the Pastor children have been arrested because of the damage they did to my car. Hopefully, when Raven is out of surgery, she'll more than likely press charges as well. Glenna has, and I'm assuming you will as well." Joey said that he would. "Good. You're in here because you have a severe concussion. Seventy-three stitches to the back of your head as well. Your leg isn't broken, but you're going to have to stay off of it for a while. It's a deep bruise to your kneecap. You were trapped under the door when the car flipped over. Christ, when I came up on that scene, I nearly had a heart attack. The wheels were still spinning, and the Pastors were trying to get out of their car and what I can only assume was to finish what they started with you three."

"The driver? Ben. Is he all right?" Caleb told him that he'd been killed when they hit the car head-on. "He was working hard to keep us from getting hurt. Did he have a family or anyone that he's leaving behind?"

"A wife but no children. He'd been setting to

retire in the coming months. William will be charged with his murder as well as the others for cheering him on. They can be heard from the street telling him to go faster and faster. And to hit the car again." Joey said that he was so sorry, and he was too. Just because they'd not gotten what they wanted from their mother. "None of the sons have a job. Besty and April's husbands have one each. April's husband has a good one, as a matter of fact. However, those men filed for divorce a few weeks ago, and Judge Martin granted them today. They won't be implicated in anything that has gone on today."

"This is a nightmare, Caleb. I don't want to even have to think about what they would have done to Glenna and Raven had they not been in the limo. The simple fact that they were in the larger car is more than likely the only thing that saved them." Caleb agreed. When Glenna was asked to go and talk to her attorney while Raven was recovering, Joey asked him what was going to happen to the young woman. "She saved Glenna from more harm. Covering her with her body when the car was spinning out of control. I have no doubt that they'd both would have been dead. I know that I said that before, but those people were out for blood."

"Not according to them." Tabby kissed Caleb, and Yazzie did the same for him when they entered the room. Then Yazzie sat down on the chair to hold his hand as she spoke to them. "They're still blaming Raven and their mom. Though I'm not sure how they figure that is going to stick. They're also saying that since they didn't mean to kill Ben, then it shouldn't count against them. Also, you'll probably not be surprised to know that they didn't have any insurance either. Not on any cars nor themselves. Again, they're blaming it on Raven and Glenna because they couldn't get to their momma's money."

"There is going to be hell to pay, I'm thinking." Tabby got up and began pacing. "I've made a couple of phone calls. One to let the president know what happened as well as calling in extra guards for the Pastor family fools. Not that I don't think that the police here can handle it, but with you down and hurt by them, I was afraid that they'd be hurt. Not that they don't deserve it, mind you. But I'm just making sure that Raven will be fine while she's recovering. She's going to get better, but she's going to take a while to do so. Especially with her leg broken. Getting away from them will be impossible if they catch her out alone sometime."

Joey was taken up to his room from the emergency room about an hour later. He was beginning to feel the pain in his head, and his body ached as well. After asking for meds to take the edge off, he lay there as still and as quietly as he could. Joey didn't know if he was going to last the night with so little in his system, but he was going to give it his best while Yazzie was still with him.

When he got word that Raven was out of surgery, he asked Yazzie to go down and check on her for him. When she returned, he knew that she'd been crying. Having her crawl into bed with him, he held her while she told him what the nurses had told her.

"She's going to be all right. They said that she'd had no trouble with the surgery or anything else that they'd given her while under." He told her that was good, and she smiled up at him, watery yes, but he was happy to see it. "I need to call her boss at some point. They handed me her cell phone that she had on her when she came in. They asked that I look at it to see if there is any family that we should call. I guess they didn't realize that I'm blind."

"Honey, people rarely notice that. But if you'll hand it to me, I'll see what I can find." He was almost too sick with the pain behind his eyes to look but did so. He knew how important it would be for him to let his wife and kids know he was all right, and he wanted to do the same for Raven. When he found the number for Palmer and Palmer, he looked at the clock while it was dialing. He was glad that it wasn't too late to be calling.

~*~

Harlin didn't mind helping out the family today. Sitting with the young woman that had nearly lost her life a few days ago was the easiest thing he'd ever done. It was making him happy that they were asking him to do something. Sitting around the house all day was making him crazy. He wasn't even sure that he could make another trip around the town without people thinking that he was casing the shops in town.

When someone knocked on the door, he was standing with his hand on his gun when the door creaked open. It was Glenna. About the most wonderful woman he'd come to meet. Well, Harlin thought, he liked them all, but she was more like he thought a grandma would have been had he had one.

"I was just bringing you in some lunch. I don't think that the hospital food here is so bad, but the cook that is at the house where I'm staying is stressful baking, she told me. I didn't have the heart to tell her that you might well have already eaten since it was so late in the afternoon." He assured her that he'd not eaten all that much and was hungry now. "Good. I'm glad. I ate one of those nice sandwiches at the house. It's really very good."

Harlin really was hungry. And as soon as he saw that it was his favorite, an Italian double meat sub, he ate half of it before he realized he was being rude. Telling Glenna that he was sorry, she smiled at him and asked him how Raven was doing today.

"Fine. But then, I don't have a lot of information on that. I mean, this is the first time that I've met her." She said that she was normally quiet, but when she had something to say, then you'd better listen. "That sounds like an attorney. I've been reading the newspaper about the accident. Your children are going to be going away for a long time, it seems. With Joey in the car, him being a federal employee, the FBI is involved to the point where they're taking over the case for the three of you. I guess their cars are being sold off for the medical expenses for this too. They didn't own their homes, not your sons, at least."

"I didn't know that either. I had it in my head that when their father passed away and left them his insurance, they were able to buy a house with that. I guess they flittered it all away like they did every dime they were given as children." Harlin slowed down eating and was glad he had when she made him laugh. "I'm sorry, son, but you don't sound to me like you laugh all that much. That's a shame, really. You have a lovely laugh."

"Thank you. And you'd be correct on that. I haven't had much of an occasion to have much in the way of good things going on in my life." She told him she was sorry for that. "I am as well. I don't want to tell you that I didn't notice it before, but since I've been here for the last few days, I've come to enjoy the laughter that seems to be in abundance in each of the households."

"I have to tell you, when they let me go back to the nursing home, I'm going to miss it too. Not just the laughter but the children here. They're the most beautiful little ones that I've ever seen." He told her how much he loved them as well. How they had accepted him like the adults had. "Yes, me as well. They're calling me Grandma Glenna. Just like that, they were taking me along to their rooms and showing me their new things. I don't think they'd had much in the way of laughter either, those little souls."

"Yes, I've heard about that as well. They're doing much better with Yazzie than I think a lot of kids do with a sighted parent. She and Joey, they sure do love those little ones. And I have to tell you, I was as surprised as I could have been to find out that they're not their biological children." The nurse came in and checked on Raven. He kept notes of her pressure as well as anything that the staff was able to tell him. The rest of his family, something that he was just getting used to calling them, would want all the information that had been there for him to observe.

"I guess the rest of them are at that meeting with the police and the FBI today. I didn't have to go because I'd been able to give my testimony the day I was brought in." Glenna sat back in her chair after reaching for Raven's hand. "She's such a good girl, this one. I have missed having her around to talk to all the time. And smart as a tack too. But not so stuck on herself that she will not be able to have a regular conversation with her."

"When Joey called her boss, he told him all sorts of things about his prized attorney, he called her. The two of you, he said, hit it off right away." Glenna said that they had. And it had been fun for them both since. "I can tell by the way that you talk about her that you're —"

Raven sat up in the bed. She stared at the two of them for several seconds before she asked him who the fuck he was. After telling her not just his name but why he was there, she laid back down.

"I thought that the idiots were here waiting to hurt me again." Glenna told her that she was so happy to see her awake. "I don't know that I am. I just heard voices and wanted to protect you. Am I going to be all right? I can see that you are. And that other man...I don't remember his name right now."

"Joey Phillips." She nodded, then cried out in pain, and Glenna held her hand tighter. "Do you need anything for it, honey? I can call those nurses in. They've been lickity split every time one of us calls for them."

"I'm hurting, but I want to be assured that you're all right." Glenna told Raven about her arm and the bruises, but before she was able to finish, Raven was asleep. He thought it was the best thing for her.

Glenna went back to Calebs, and he sat there with the young woman and read the rest of the newspaper articles about the Pastor children. There was a bit about them on every page, it seemed. Even though they were all grown adults, the newspaper called them children as well. Like they were ten-year-olds in grown-up bodies.

He was just finishing the last article when Raven asked him his name again. After telling her, he took her hand when she reached for his. Holding her, he was happy to be able to tell her that Glenna was all right really and that Joey was mending at home.

"Those fools tried to kill us." He said that the newspaper had a great article about them. "I'm sure that it's wonderful. But doesn't get all their stupidity down. I've been working against them for the last ten years. It's always comes down to the same thing. Money. Are you wealthy?"

The change of subject didn't bother him. He was sort of used to it being in the service. It was a good way to keep a person on their toes as well as keeping focused on what was going on in front of him. Shaking his head, he realized that her eyes were closed and answered her verbally.

"No. I don't have a pot to piss in, as the saying goes." She said that she was considered wealthy but didn't think she was. "You want more money than you have now?"

"No, it's not that. I just don't think that money means all that much to me. I know how that sounded, but I don't buy a lot of crap. I have a condo that I've had since I was seventeen. It looks pretty much the same as it did when I purchased it. Except I have a bed now instead of an air mattress. I don't own a television. I don't own any books, but I get what I want to read from the library. I do have some law books that I've kept over the years, but they were all second-hand. I have four skirts, six blouses as well as two jackets that match it all. I'm not what people would call a shopper. I hate going to the mall. Detest eating alone, and I have one friend, and she's old enough to be my great grandma."

"You have any family? Parents? Brothers or sisters?" She told him that she had a sister, but she was killed by domestic abuse on her honeymoon. A brother that had overdosed when he was twelve, and her parents were both in prison for his death. "I'm sorry to hear that. I truly am."

"It's all right, I guess." She told him, too, that she needed something for pain. "I'm starting to feel every part of my body that has been abused. Do you think you can have them hurry things up for me?"

"I can do that." He pressed the button on the call cord near her bed. After telling the woman that answered that Raven needed some pain medication, Raven asked if she could have a small sip of water. The nurse said that she could have ice chips. "I'll help feed them to you when she brings them in."

Raven's face was covered up for the most part. Her eyes were beautiful, but they, too, were bruised and bloodied. When she drifted off, much slower than he had thought she should have, he watched her for a long while as she breathed in and out. It was almost putting him to sleep, watching her when he remembered to make notes on what they spoke about and how long she'd been awake. Looking at the clock in the room, he realized that he'd been here for seven hours and that it didn't feel like it. He'd actually enjoyed watching over Raven, and he'd do it anytime they needed him to do it in the future too.

At six-thirty, Tabby and Caleb showed up. After telling them what had happened today with Raven and Glenna, they told him that they were taking him to dinner. It was going to be Joey, with his broken leg coming in to watch over her.

"He has another appointment to get x-rays of his knee. They want to keep on top of it in case it starts to swell more. Or if he might need surgery." Harlin asked if he was going to be all right in here alone. "That man would be able to fend off an army with one gun if asked to do so. I think he feels slightly responsible for what happened, and he'd not been able to keep Glenna and Raven from being hurt. I'm thrilled that none of them were killed. Are you ready to go, Harlin?"

Harlin wanted to stay. In fact, he was sort of upset that he wouldn't be able to. But he left with them and went to the restaurant they'd had reservations at. Joey had only just shown up when they were leaving, and he had his laptop as well as one of his children to keep him company. His wife was coming in later to spell him for a while.

Harlin was enjoying his time here with the family he now had, but he wondered how much longer they'd be putting him up since he had no money, no job, and he didn't have any idea what to do with his life now. He said as much to Caleb when Tabby went to the ladies' room.

"You're going to be fine. Right now, I want you to be rested up and feeling better. You've been handed a lot in the last few days, and I think you're starting to look better. You look less like you're hurting too. Am I right on that?"

"Yes. I don't feel any pressure, either. I hadn't realized that I was feeling that until this morning when I got up. And that bed that I'm using Christ, I'd carry that on my back to everywhere I went if I could get away with it." They both laughed, and Tabby returned. "I was just telling Caleb how nice the bed is. I've been sleeping in my car for a while now. Then the bed at my mother's home wasn't the best either."

They spoke about the house that he was going to look at tomorrow. Harlin was worried a little about how big the house was going to be. He'd seen the others, and it made him nervous to think that he might end up with a house with ten bedrooms and a family to fill it. Harlin wasn't sure at this point if he was ready for his own family or not. But he supposed time would tell.

Chapter 3

Donald James couldn't understand why they were charging them all for the murder of the limo driver. The only person that had been driving was William Hunter. And for as much as he loved his older brother, he didn't like him all that much either. Not even to go to jail with him. Besides, it had been his idea to kill off Blackbird anyway. So that they'd be able to take care of their momma. Not that he really wanted to.

He loved his momma. Very much. But there was a limit even he couldn't cross. And taking care of her needs, like changing her diaper — he'd not ever done it to his kids. He certainly didn't want to do that for his momma. No way, no how. Donald James thought about it and wondered if she did indeed wear those things. Not that it mattered. There were other things going on that he couldn't be watching his momma.

His wife, Lisa—she never would tell him her middle name—told him that if they won the case and that his momma had to come and live with them, she was going to leave. There were plenty of other members of their family that had room to put her in, she told him. They only had a three-bedroom home, and their daughters, all three of them, were bunked into one of them. Donald James shared one with his wife, and the third bedroom was for when they had guests over.

First of all, he didn't remember a single time that they ever had a guest over that ended up staying the night. Secondly, that room looked better than the one that he had. Then there was the furniture. He wished all the time he'd done what Betsy Sue had done and buy new furniture with her winnings after their daddy died, and they'd been given insurance money. Donald knew that it wasn't winnings but insurance; however, she'd had some really nice stuff until her husband got a burr up his ass and didn't allow them to come over no more to spend some time drinking and being with their sister.

Not that it mattered all that much now. All

of them had lost the stuff they'd had in the homes that they'd been renting, except for Besty Sue and April Showers. But then they'd lost their homes, too, on account of their husbands being too good for them. That's what he'd been told by them that had happened.

As he thought on it, he realized that spending his winnings on a nice vacation with his wife and kids had been a better idea than furniture that was going to be sold off for money to give to the courts. That brought him right around again to why he was in jail. Looking over at his brother when he said his name, Donald James wasn't in the mood to hear him bitching again and told him that.

"You'll listen because I told you to. Did you get a chance to call Momma yet? I tried, but the number I had is saying that it's been turned off. You thinking that that Blackbird woman took all her money and Momma got her phone shut off?" For some reason, Donald James doubted that the woman, Blackbird — what they'd been calling her forever — needed the money. He told William Hunter that. "Everyone needs money, you moron. Even if I had it all, and I will someday, you wait and see, I'd want more of it. You can't ever have enough green stuff. What makes you think she don't need the money?"

"She's an attorney? Duh. Her clothes. She had some fancy stuff on when we was in court with her. And that computer. I thought that the only way to use one was to have it plugged in all the time. But there she was with it sitting on her desk, not plugged in." He laughed a little. "That's what Betsy Sue was going for when they finally stopped trying to run from us. That's another thing that I don't understand either. Where did that big car come from? Blackbird and Momma only came there in that little bitty thing that Blackbird drove. I saw it in the parking lot when we got there."

"I don't know, but I'm not thinking that it belongs to that stupid bitch." Donald turned back towards the hall. There wasn't anything out there, but it was better than looking at William Hunter lying on his bed naked. "You didn't answer me. Did you get in touch with Momma?"

"No. You just told me that her number has been disconnected. How do you expect me to be able to call her when you couldn't?" He wanted to hit his brother but stayed where he was. "You tell me again why you thought it was a good idea to kill off Blackbird. As far as I can see, you did nothing right, and we're all in jail for it. And I don't understand that either. Why we're in jail with you."

He was poking the bear. He knew it. But Donald James was bored, and when he was bored, he did stupid things. He supposed that the old saying of idle hands gets your ass into trouble was right. There sure was going to be trouble if he kept at what he was doing to William Hunter.

"Because I told that attorney fella that we was a family and that was how we was going to get out of here. You'll see. With us all being together, they'll have to split up our sentence if there is one between the four of us. It'll be shorter. Dummy head. Plus, without the stupid attorney around, Momma would have to live with us. Don't you see?" Donald told him that he didn't see that working. They just got her another attorney when Blackbird had been hurt. "No, no. They wouldn't have fought so much in not letting her live with us. They would have been glad to have her out of the way."

It didn't make any sense to him what William Hunter was saying, but he kept his mouth shut. Lunch was coming, and he was hungry. He didn't know what they had fixed up for them, but since breakfast was so good and last night's dinner had been wonderful, lunch had to be just as good. But the cop was telling William Hunter if he didn't get himself dressed, they weren't going to get their trays.

"I'm not naked. Hand mine over, and I promise you I'll not share." The cop stood there with both trays in his hand, shaking his head. "Please. I'm powerful hungry. He does that all the time on account of him saying that he's too hot for wearing clothes like regular people. He said that he was made hotter than other normal people. Just give me my food, and I'll eat it while you stand there so you can see that I'll not share."

"Put your clothing on, Mr. Pastor, or I'm going to have to have them put on you." That didn't sound so much like he was going to be nice about helping him put them on, and Donald James got off his bed and rolled to the floor. There was going to be some bloodshed, and he wanted not a thing to do with it. "Did you hear me? I said for you to get dressed."

"I'm working on it." No, he wasn't. William Hunter was taking his time with it, and it was starting to piss him off. "Donald James, come here and help me with my britches."

"No, sir. You're naked, and I want nothing to do with your nasty body." Donald James stayed where he was, sitting on his hands, too, so that he'd not get into trouble. "Just get yourself dressed, William Hunter, so's I can eat. Hurry up before he goes and gets some of them big fellers and helps you. Do you want to end up in the hospital again for not listening to the police?"

"I'm getting there." He finally sat up and pulled his pants up to his thighs. When that wasn't enough for the cop, he pulled his shirt over his head and stood up to fix his pants. Christ, oh mighty Donald James thought he was going to starve near to death before his stupid brother finished with the zipper. "You'd think you'd never seen a naked person before. It's just like your body."

"Nobody has a body that looks like your body, Mr. Pastor. Here. Take your meals. And if I come back here again and you're not clothed, I'm going to run your brother to the other end of the hall, and you won't be able to speak to him." He took his meal, thinking that he might enjoy being at the other end of the hall. William Hunter stank. Not only that, but he was a nasty sort of person too. Forever playing with his dick and balls like there was a match going on, and he was set to win.

His meal was better than he'd thought it might

have been. There were peas and carrots with lots of butter on them. As well as three thick slices of meatloaf with bacon and ketchup all over the top of it. There was a nice-sized bowl of mashed-up taters and a couple of slices of white bread. Making him a meatloaf sammich. He was done with it before his brother was naked again on the bed. Turning his back to his brother so he'd not have to look at him, Donald James enjoyed his meal.

After he ate, he unwrapped the large hunk of Angle food cake. It had those crispy pieces on it, just like he loved. As he was breaking it off and shoving it into his mouth, the cop came by again and told him to stand up. Putting the last of it in his mouth, he did just what he'd been told to do. That was to back against the wall behind him. Of course, William Hunter had to bitch about that too. Even though it had not a thing to do with him.

"I'm not going to be happy if you take my brother down the hall. It's not right. And I know my rights." The officer pointed out that he was naked again and that they all had the rights not to have to see him in the nude like he was. When the door was opened, and he was told to come along, he did so without a word. William Hunter was still complaining about him going away wasn't fair to him. "Donald James, you tell them that you don't want to go nowhere. I'm telling you right now, you'd better be getting back in here, or I'm going to be hurting you."

He didn't say a word but followed the officer down the hall. When he got there, still being a good prisoner, he was told that they had an extra meal and that it was his if he wanted it. Even though he was full to his tonsils, he told him he'd love it. Making him another sammich, he was enjoying it when he saw the four big officers dragging a hose down the hall to where he'd been with William Hunter.

Not that he wanted any part of William Hunter getting in trouble, he did wish that he could have seen his face when they turned the water on. It sprayed him a bit when the hose got a little kinked up, but he was enjoying the sounds that his brother was making as the water was hitting him. He was surely cursing up a blue streak, as his daddy used to say all the time.

Telling him that he was going to be wearing his clothes from now on and not to take them off had William Hunter cursing like a sailor again. Donald didn't know what that saying had ever meant, but his daddy had said it all the time too. Listening to a little tune in his head as he enjoyed his second meal, he was up on his bed when the hose was being dragged back from his brother's cell. Nobody said he had to go back, and he was happy about that as a meadowlark in the summer.

Closing his eyes, slightly uncomfortable from eating so much, he thought about all the shit that had been going on since he'd been old enough to remember. Not that he was a good person, he knew he wasn't, but William Hunter and April Showers, being the oldest two, had been making plans since they'd been born, he thought. Just to get into trouble.

The first plan that they'd made was just before school started when they was little. Not that he nor Betsy Sue had been old enough to go yet, but they'd been in the plan too. April Showers had said that it was only fair as they were going to be getting out of going to school the same as they were. Not that he ever understood how that was going to work. Even as a kid, he knew that there were a whole lot of buses, and them letting all the air out of the tires on the one that was to come for them wasn't going to be enough. But he kept his mouth shut and wasn't surprised when they were hauled off to school when they were supposed to be picked up, even on the same bus.

There were other things, too, that they'd plot and plan. Like the summer their momma had put up a great big bunch of peaches. While he'd been the lookout, William Hunter had taken four dozen of the filled jars out into the cornfield and had busted them all to pieces. He didn't even take the peaches out for eating but just smashed them all to mush with his foot.

He'd cut himself badly doing that. They'd all had to carry his sorry ass all the way back to the house while he bled like he'd been stuck with a kitchen knife. Then, Momma, being pissed off about the peaches, she took him to the hospital and didn't allow them to give him any pain medication while they stitched him up. Daddy had been so angry that night that he'd put their momma in the hospital. Donald James had missed his momma more than he did his brother.

When he thought about his momma, Donald James didn't think of her the way the others had. Nobody but him and his momma knew it, but Donald James would get her some flowers from the field behind the house on Mother's Day. He'd also be the only one that would make her a present in art class at school for Christmas. He even went so far as to make the Thanksgiving decorations for the table too. It was always William Hunter and the girls that complained about what they got from their momma. He'd known that she was the one getting them for them. Using her sewing money to do so too. His mom could make a shirt out of near nothing when he'd been a kid.

There was other things, too, that he thought about. His daddy. Daddy would beat Momma so bad a couple of times a month that would send her away in an ambulance. That didn't mean that he didn't smack on her all the rest of the time. It was just far worse when he got drunk.

Donald James rolled to his back and thought of his parents. His daddy had told them that they needed to keep their wives in line when they married by making sure that they knew who the boss was. But he told the girls that they needed to stand up for themselves so that their husbands didn't beat them too much. Donald James had never hit his wife. Nor his kids. He didn't even like it when Lisa beat their butts when they needed it.

There was money coming into his home, unlike his brother and sisters. Or there had been. He didn't know what was going to happen to that. Lisa had helped him apply for social security when she'd married him because of him being so stupid. She'd not ever called him that, but he knew that's what it meant when they were told that he had a very low IQ. He probably could have told them that when they did the tests, but they wouldn't have forked over the money had he suggested that. Lisa would put good food on the table and a bit back for birthdays, she told him. He wondered if the courts were going to get all that money too.

He hated hurting his momma. Donald James hadn't been treated like the others had growing up. Momma told him that he was delicate. He didn't ask anyone what that meant. He was sort of afraid to find out what the answer might be. But he let her call him that. Especially late at night when he'd find her in the kitchen crying so quietly it was like the squeak of a little bitty mouse.

"Oh, Donald." She was the only one that called him that. Momma called the others by their first and middle name but not him. He'd been told once that it made it sound like you was from the middle of nowhere. He was, but he didn't point that out to people. "What am I going to do now? With your daddy dead, there isn't anyone to keep the others from killing me. And they'll try. You might even too, but I can't protect myself and try to make a living on top of that."

They were all grown by then. Daddy had gone to bed one night after beating Momma and hadn't woke up. Not that he ever hit on them, but Donald James was glad that he was gone. He wasn't a good person to anyone. His yelling at them all the time, telling them how stupid they were, got on his nerves some. Yes, he thought now. He was glad that his daddy was gone.

Momma had been hurt bad once. She told everyone that she'd fallen, but he thought that his sisters and brothers had knocked her down. A broken hip, the doctor told them, wouldn't heal right without proper care. All the others wanted to know was when she was going to be home fixing them food and washing up their clothes. Momma was put in a nursing home the following week. He thought that had been a good place for her to heal and to rest up. However, she never came home again.

"Mr. Pastor?" He told the man standing at the cell in front of him that it was him. "I'm here to serve you with paperwork. You don't have to sign anything, but you will need to take it from me."

"All righty." He got up, still feeling a bit off from his big meals. He took the paperwork from the man. "I can't sign my name, so I couldn't of done that anyway. I can't read either. Do you have somebody to come here and read this to me?"

"I can send someone." When the man turned and left, he sat down on the cot again. What he wouldn't give for just a chair. It didn't even have to be one of those reclining things. Just a normal chair. Sitting around all the time was making his back act up again. But he'd not ask. He wasn't going to make it so he was hosed down.

Sometime later, he didn't know the times anymore. Someone came to read the paperwork to him. He could tell where the hands were pointed, but that didn't help him much if they were too close together. Following the officer that was going to read the things to him that he'd been served with, he didn't say a word, not even when he was curious about who would be sending him something to read.

~*~

Raven wasn't feeling great, but she was feeling a good deal better than she had been. This morning they'd put her in a chair and had given her the computer that she'd had in the limo. However, it was busted all up, and she couldn't see the screen anymore. Mr. Palmer was going to send her another one to use, and she was happy about that.

"Hello." She turned slowly to look at the man standing there. It was Harlin again. She wanted to smile at him, glad to see him, but her face was still too tight with stitches and swelling. However, she did tell him how happy she was to see him. "They said you could have some light meals. I brought you some chicken broth. There is also some rice in it, they said it would do you good to have some of that. Are you hungry?"

"I am, as a matter of fact." He sat the thermos in front of her and pulled a bowl out of the bag as well. There were even crackers, but he hadn't checked if she could have those, so he called for the nurse. When it was okayed for her to have a few crackers and the bottled water that he'd brought, she let him wait on her by putting a large napkin over her lap as well as one tucked into her gown under her chin. There was also pepper for her to sprinkle lightly she'd been told in the soup of she wanted it. "I guess they're afraid of me sneezing or something. I had a client that had been hurt in the face, and when he sneezed, they had to redo all his stitches."

"I thought that it might be too spicy for your cuts in your mouth. What you said makes more sense. Just be super careful with the soup. It's almost as hot as when it was made." She was careful. Not just with the crackers, which she thought tasted like heaven might, but she also didn't slurp. That, too, would pull the stitches. "I'm going to talk to you while you eat if you have no objection." She told him to go ahead. "I have a house now. I mean, I think some people would call it a mansion, but I have a place of my own, thanks to Caleb. He purchased all of us — his half-brothers — a home, and we're all to pick out which one we want. Since I was forth coming here, there are two houses left."

"I've read up on him. He's an extremely wealthy man." She was enjoying the soup so much that she finished it off before she realized it. "I'm not stuffed, but I certainly feel better than I did before you arrived. Thank you for thinking of me."

"I don't mind at all. I have a cook. Staff too. Though I have no idea why. I'm just going along with the flow of things and not asking too many questions. I'm sure that I could, and no one would say anything, but it's been good to just let others boss me around. For now, anyway." He laughed a little, and she was close to laughing with him. "The women are the ones that boss me around the most, I guess. Tabby and the others, they just want me to feel better. To be honest, I wasn't feeling all that great when I got here. But now I feel better than I thought that I haven't in a while. Felt good, I mean."

"I didn't feel too bad when I got up. But after they moved me to here, I felt like I'd been hurt all over again. However, after just taking a pain reliever, I do feel good. I didn't realize how hungry I was until I opened the soup." He told her that he was having beef stew with bread for dinner. "Well, that's not nice to tell me about that. I love soups. No matter what kind."

"I'll bring you some in the morning. Even some bread. That way, you can sop up the juices with it. The staff told me that if I wanted, I could leave you things here, and they'll heat them up for you. All you need to do is ask for it, and they'll bring it hot and steamy to you." She said that she'd kill for a bowl of popcorn. "Oh, that does sound good. When you're released from here and getting around better, we'll go to the movies just for the popcorn."

"Are you asking me out?" He looked confused

just for a second, then he nodded with a huge smile on his face. "Good. If you didn't get around to it, I was going to have to ask you out. I like spending time with you."

"I do you as well." She enjoyed his company. To the point where if anyone showed up while they were together, she wanted to ask them to go away. He was bright, shy, and he seemed to understand her when she would rant. Something that she did quite often while laid up. "Speaking of going home, they're going to let me leave when I have a situation set up. I'd never heard of a place to live that is safe to live called that, but I'm glad for it. Caleb said he'd hire me a nurse. It'll be covered as part of the insurance with the accident. I know that I'd feel better where someone could keep an eye on me rather than my place. It's mostly empty, so I could get around, but I'd have to figure out a way to get up the four flights of stairs to even get in the door."

"Stay with me." She looked at him, and he seemed to be embarrassed. "I only have myself around. There is a staff, as I said, but it's a big flipping house. The master suite is on the first floor, but there are ten bedrooms on the second floor."

"Good lord. You did say that the houses were

large." Leaning back in the chair she was in, she thought about living in his house. Not with him but in the house. "I think I might take you up on staying with you. Joey told me that Caleb's home is really nice, but it's always noisy. Joey's home is full of kids. While I've nothing against children, I don't know how good I'd be around them. And Martin and his wife — what's her name?" He told her. "Right. Gracie, they're still in their honeymoon stages, and I'm afraid of them shoving me off the couch to have at it again."

They both laughed. Raven had noticed that it came easier to Harlin than it had before. It was also heartier. Like he meant it. Not that she thought he'd fake laughter, but more like he wasn't used to it, and he'd have to remember how to do it again. As they talked about her staying with him — her making it clear that it was staying at the house and not living with him, she was excited to leave the hospital. Not that anyone had ever been anything but kind and helpful to her, but she wanted her own space and her own things around her.

"Oh. I nearly forgot. Glenna is going back to the nursing home tomorrow. I'm not sure if she's very keen on the idea or not. She has really enjoyed her time being free, she told me. I think that the only reason that she was in the nursing home in the first place was to get away from her family. Am I right in assuming that?" She told him about how Glenna had broken her hip when she'd first ended up in the home. But she had liked the safeness of it so much that she stayed. "My mother was a horrible person most of the time. Then my father would come along and make it worse for us both. He's the biological father to the four of us men, as well as the other two that are coming. Caleb has worked hard in getting us all found so that he could help us out. He's a good man."

"He is. He's frightfully wealthy, but he doesn't act like it." Harlin asked her how much was frightfully wealthy. "Billions upon billions of dollars. Land and businesses as well. The man that wrote the article about him and Tabby said that it was incalculable the amount of money he has. That, to me, is a frightful amount of money."

"I think it would be for me as well." They spoke about what they'd do with that much money. After saying a few things and Harlin telling her that he had them, like a private jet as well as homes all over the world, they couldn't think of a single thing to buy. "I guess you'd get to that point. Helping others out, too, he does do that a great deal. I'm not counting his half-brothers in that. But he does things for the local economy as well as the schools and elderly homes. I'd like to think that was something that I'd do, but I also think that I'd be afraid to spend much of it. I'd be wanting to keep it all for a rainy day. I guess it would have to flood for me to have to use it all, but I'd have it. What about you?"

"I grew up with money, so I'm better at spending it if I need to. I don't, just so you know. I'm as tight-fisted as my grannie was. But when my brother died, I told you about him. I think my parents figured out that no amount of money would bring him back, and they just stopped spending it on anything. Not even to make their lives better on the inside. When Paula was murdered a few years later, it was just too much for them, and they stopped buying the necessities as well. They were looking pretty bad when I went to see them last time. And that was when they told me not to come there anymore. They're supposed to get out next year, but I'm afraid that they'll not try just because the world has become too much for them."

"That's really sad for them. Losing two children in the space of a few years, I think it would make me crawl into myself as well." Raven told Harlin about her brother and sister while they relaxed. "Your brother was your twin? I hadn't any idea. Though I don't know why I'd know that." He laughed again. "So you were both very young when he died. And being a twin, it must have hurt you twice as badly." She nodded and told him that it felt like she was just getting over him dying, her parents going to prison when her sister was killed on her honeymoon. "Is her husband still in jail?"

"No. He ended up killing himself in his jail cell before he was taken to court and found guilty. The fucker. None of us had any idea that he'd been knocking my sister around before that. It turned out to be drugs. My parents, of course, blamed that on themselves as well because they weren't there when she needed them." Raven thought of her identifying her sister that day. "Samuel had blunged her so badly that I could barely recognize her. If not for the scar that she had on her left leg, I doubt I could have said who she was. They did confirm it with dental records, but even that was hard to do with the damage that had been done to her."

"I'm so sorry for your loss, Raven." He took her hand into his much larger one, and they were quiet for a while. When Glenna showed up, bringing cookies for her to share with the elderly woman, she didn't let go of his hand. Nor did he seem inclined to let hers go either.

"Do you really like living in the nursing home, Glenna?" Startled by the question, Glenna asked him what he meant. "I was just asking you if you liked living there. You've had so much fun, I think, being out and about all on your own. I can understand a bit of that. Your children aren't around to hurt you. But I think, and this could just be me, that you've not been looking forward to goin back as much as you did when you won your case. Are you?"

"Not really. I've tried to be excited about it again. But I will admit that I'm going to miss the children. And the adults too. It's been wonderful for me to be able to take a walk down the street and talk to people. Going in and out of shops when I want. There isn't anyone making me hurry through it either because I'm not holding up the bus. Even going down to the ice cream place and having myself some of those Frenchie fries is a wonderful feeling." Harlin looked at her. She knew just where he was going and couldn't have been more happy than she was at that moment. He then asked Glenna if she'd live with the two of them. "The two of you, you say?

Well, I don't know. Is this a long-term invite, or are you two just funning with an old woman."

"I don't know any old women. But I think that, with Raven living there in the house that I own and you there, a man couldn't ask for a better arrangement than having two of the most beautiful women he's ever seen around all the time." Glenna was embarrassed and smacked Harlin on the arm gently. "I'm serious. Raven is going to need a place she can live that will keep her from falling down stairs. My brother gifted me a lovely large home that would be perfect for the three of us. Even long-term. There is a nice paddock out back that I was thinking would be a good place to stable horses. Or raise pigs. A big barn that is heated and air-conditioned that I think would be perfect for any projects that the two of you might have in mind. Also, I know for a fact that one of the upper bedrooms has an adjoining room that would be perfect for your sewing room. A lot of plugs on each wall and windows all around it so that you can see your work. Also, I didn't mention this before I asked Raven to stay there, but there is a beautiful gilded elevator that will be perfect for taking my two lovely ladies to the upper floor if that's what you want."

"Don't get this old lady's hopes up for nothing, young man." He told her that he'd never do that. Not to anyone. Dashing one's hopes was just cruel, he told her. Glenna looked at her. "What do you think about this? Having me there will be hard when I get older."

"You have some years left before I think of you being older. We'll work up to that when the time comes. I think this is an excellent idea. And we'll make the house safe for you when it's time. But that's far off in the future, Glenna. Far-far off, I hope." She reached for Harlin's hand again, and he took it, squeezing it tightly. However, when he kissed the back of it, she felt a fluttering all the way to her toes. "We'll have to celebrate when I get out of here. I'm looking forward to it more than I did before. And I can work from there if necessary. Caleb asked me to go over a few bits of paperwork for him, and now I'm excited about that as well."

"I'm going to do it." Glenna looked at Harlin. "I think I'm going to adopt the two of you as my children. Yes. I think that's exactly what I'm going to do."

They had plenty to square away before Glenna was able to live with the two of them. There would also be her checks too. Not that she cared if she paid them a dime while living there, but that would be up to Harlin. It was his house, after all. They decided that there was no time like the present, and Harlin went to pick them up malts for their first of many meals, she hoped. She could have one of those, and it would help with her calories.

While he was gone, she went over a couple of things with Glenna. Telling her so long as she had money, her money was her own to do with what she wanted. She had to turn away when the tears started flowing down her cheeks, and Raven was all right with that. Time would tell what Harlin wanted to do now that he had the two of them staying at his home. As they were just getting notes together on things that had to be taken care of, mostly for Glenna, Harlin showed up with not just malts, but he had French fries for Glenna and cheese and crackers for her.

"If you keep this up, I might well fall in love with you." If she hadn't been looking at him, she might have missed the look of hope on his face. "Do you care if I fall in love with you, Harlin?"

"Not at all. That would put us on the same page. I think I've been in love with you since I first got a chance to watch over you." Embarrassed herself, she lowered her head and dug into her food. Harlin was so nice that he spoke to Glenna while she had time to get herself gathered up.

No one had ever said those words to her before. Not even her parents that she could remember after all this time. But when Harlin said that he loved her, Raven couldn't help but feel like she was in a dream and that everything was going to be all right.

And it would be all right too, she just realized. She'd have a good life with Harlin and the family that he had. She might even go and see her parents again when they were set up. Just to give them some good news and to allow them to meet a good man. One that she knew deep in her heart would never harm her. Verbally nor physically.

When Glenna left to go back to Calebs, Harlin helped her make arrangements to have their home inspected for Glenna to live there. It wasn't necessary, but she felt like the courts would look at them better if they were willing to go the extra mile with her. She also asked him about Glenna's money.

"I don't want her money to live with us. Not at all. As I said, I don't have anything right now, but I'm going to be working with Caleb on some things he has going, and that'll be enough, I think to get us by. With no house payment, I don't believe we'll have to work ourselves to the bone to live there. But then, I've never owned a house before." They both laughed, and she asked if she could take care of that part for them. "Yes. I'd like it better, too, if your name was on the deed as well. Just so in the event, something happens to me, you'll be able to — I'm not saying it will. But I have to look out for the two of you, and it would make me a happy man to have you sign off on the deed as Raven Bentley."

"Are you asking me to marry you too?" She'd been joking, but he nodded and got down on one knee. Handing her a ring that looked as if he'd gotten it out of a gumball machine. She couldn't have asked for a better engagement ring. "It's perfect. Just perfect for our marriage."

He *had* gotten it from the gumball machine at the ice cream place where he'd gotten them the malts and fries. Also, and this made her laugh all the more, he'd been going for a piece of gum and was surprised when the ring had been in the machine full of colorful balls of bubble gum. She took it as a good sign. A very good sign for the three of them.

Chapter 4

Harlin tried to get a sense of what was going on in their back yard. Not that he didn't know, really, but it was difficult to wrap his head around it. The barn, after a quick inspection by him and Raven, had a great many things in it that the police, as well as any other officially initialized group from the government, were interested in. It had Caleb laughing but he and Raven, not so much.

"It's not going to come back on either of you. Even Raven told you that. I hate to say this, Harlin, but you need to relax a little. I'm worried about you." He said that it was a great deal to worry about but sat down when he was told. A chair had been brought out just for him. "I just can't believe that all this sat here for the twelve or so years before I purchased the place. And no one had called the police for the missing people. That's what boggles my mind the most. That there are people missing, and no one seemed to care all that much." Harlin said that there were body parts in the barn. "Yes. You've no idea how sorry I am that it wasn't looked into before you guys started moving in."

The inspector for the house had finished up and gone away before he had taken a walk out to the big barn. They had spoken about moving her office into the place so that she could step away from it when she needed a break. He was going to make sure that it was fit for that and that internet could be brought to it. However, this? This right here? Well, he wanted the sucker torn down and never spoken of again. Harlin watched as one of the agents with FBI on their vest that was first on the scene came toward him and Caleb.

It occurred to him that everyone was being really nice. Some were disgusted by what they had unearthed, while others took it in stride. He did have to wonder about their life up until today if the image of an old blood-covered electric saw and jars of body parts didn't make them even blink hard. It made him shudder every time he thought about what they'd found.

"You said that you entered the building through the side door." He told the officer that he had but had opened the front sliding door when he couldn't find any switches to turn on the lights. "I hate to ask you this again, Harlin, but what was it you saw first that alerted you to knowing that this was a crime scene? I mean, you've told us several times. But I want you to think hard about what you did first. Like, did you touch anything else but the doors? Did you go to the back of the barn before calling us?"

"I didn't see anything at first. I was looking up at the rafters wondering—stupidly, I guess—who had been climbing the ladders that put those boards up that high. Then when my eyes adjusted to the darkness of the barn, all I saw was an ungodly amount of trash bags." He closed his eyes for just a moment. "They were stacked up. Like sandbags when there is a chance of a flood. All black but a single one right in the middle. Now that I think about it, I think it was to draw your attention to that. It was white, you see. In a sea of black, it was the only one that wasn't." He looked at the agent. "That's when I thought I saw what looked like a hand pressed up against the material that the bag was made of."

"All right." As the agent continued to write

things down, he noticed that Raven was talking to another agent. He figured that they were more than likely going to compare what the two of them had to say. He'd called her to get in her wheelchair, a brand new motorized one and come out to him. "Raven was upset that Caleb had paid for someone's trash. She was going to find who he bought the house from and demand that they pay for the bags to be hauled away. Then after a few seconds of her talking, she went quiet. I turned to where she was looking, and she was standing in front of the bag with the hand."

"Did you know that it was a human hand?" Harlin just glared at the man. "Look, Harlin. We have, after only opening three of the over sixty bags in there with body parts of a single dead person in each one of them, over sixty. Then just as I was thinking that it couldn't get any worse, one of the men found that the barn has a basement in it. A fucking basement that has another stack of bags. Filled, it was confirmed with more body parts. Some of them dating back to when this barn was built, we're thinking. Please cut me some slack, as I'm about as green as I've ever been to something like this."

"I'm sorry." The agent, he only knew his last name was Doughtery nodded. "It's been a lot for us to take in as well. We just started moving in this morning. My wife's very good friend is coming from the nursing home this afternoon with her things to live with us. The county inspector for our home, one that has to okay Glenna living with us, just left. Christ."

"You're going to be all right, Harlin." Nodding while Caleb pushed his head down to his knees, he heard Caleb talking to the agent. "I'm to understand that the house will need to be gone over as well. You have our full cooperation on this and anything else that you need. Your boss called me directly and said that whatever you need, you just tell me, and I'll get it for you. Whatever it is."

"Giving us the paperwork on who you bought the land and buildings from was very helpful. Mr. Cleary was the last owner before the bank took it over, so we're going to start there." Caleb said that he was dead. "Yes, I thought as much. But we're going to have to talk to whatever family is left to find out what they know about this."

"I understand too that you guys are going to help us out with getting this cleaned up when it's finished here, correct?" Harlin noticed the way the agent didn't look at him but far off in the distance.

Harlin asked again. "You're not saying anything. Am I to assume that something else has come up during this investigation?"

"It might take us years to process this, Harlin. I'm being serious when I tell you, I'm thinking that I'll be dead and dust myself before this is finished up. There is just so much we can process in a day. With this? I'm thinking that it will take us a decade just to get through the equipment that is in there. Then there are the bodies." Harlin felt his head spinning again. He'd only found out recently that he had high blood pressure, and today's events were testing the medication he'd been taking. "Everything, and I'm thinking that they'll include the house, will be taken apart board by board and gone over. You and your new family won't be able to live here while that is going on. I'm so sorry. This is a major crime scene, and I don't see this getting finalized for decades."

"Christ." He'd said that so many times today that he decided that he wasn't going to say it anymore. It helped to be able to say something, but that word, with all this shit, wasn't cutting it. He also thought that it was overused too. Putting his head back between his knees to let his head get settled, he wondered what he was going to do now. Where were they going to live? For that matter, what happens to the things that they'd already taken in the house. He asked the man that. "I mean, it wasn't much. Just some linens and a box of pots and pans. We had ordered what we wanted online but wanted to eat here — I don't even think I could use those things now that I think about it. Never mind. I don't want it."

They were told that they were being put up in a nice hotel for the night. Caleb said that they'd take them home with him and have a nice dinner. Right now, he wasn't sure that he could eat, but he thought that being with Caleb and his family would be better than being able to think at a hotel. He'd just as soon never think of this again.

Another agent called for Doughtery, and he left them. While he and Caleb were making arrangements for them to go to their home, Agent Doughtery came back. He asked him if they'd been to the basement. At all.

"No." He just caught himself saying 'Christ' again. "Please tell me what it is you found down there that you have to ask me that? Am I ever going to be able to go into a barn or basement again without having the willies?"

"The barn is still being used, Harlin." Getting

up and sitting down twice was all it took to get him moving to find Raven. She was his wife as of this morning, thanks to having the paperwork filed as all the others had done. Neither of them had any family to speak of, and Raven was more than happy with those arrangements. As soon as he was close enough to touch her, he hugged her and then nearly dragged her in her wheelchair to their car. It was enough. More than enough to have him regretting ever coming to this town.

He drove. But it was her telling him that if he didn't relax and soon, she was going to take him to the emergency department. He was looking bad. Harlin wasn't sure what she was comparing his looks to but kept his mouth shut. When he pulled over into one of the parks that Caleb's mom had had built, he watched the children playing before he felt calm enough to speak.

"We won't be able to live there. The agent said it would be decades before it was finalized." She didn't say anything, so he continued with what he'd been told and his thoughts on it. "Someone is still using the basement he told me. It's been going on right under our noses, and we hadn't any idea."

"I grew up around here. I never would have

thought that it was going on." He turned and looked at her while he leaned his head back on the seat. "The couple that lived there were odd. I guess that's an understatement now that I know a little of what was going on there. They didn't have any children. At least, that I'm aware of. One thought that kept coming to mind while I was talking to the agents that I can't get out of my head was that they had the most beautiful flower gardens all around the house and barn. My mom asked Mrs. Cleary once how she did it, and she told us that it was all in the way they took care that the ground was well as using lots of fertilizer. That's all I could think of while standing there. Fertilizer."

Harlin looked at Raven and felt laughter coming from his belly. He didn't even try to stifle it but let it go. It was that, or he was going to have his head explode just thinking about how the pretty little flowers in the yard were more than likely so nice because of all the blood and whatever else they didn't keep was put in the ground. When he was calm enough to stop and think again, he reached for Raven's hand and held it.

"We'll have to find us another place to live. One with plenty of room for the three of us. Also,

I didn't ask, but did you want any children? I don't have a preference either way, but I think I'd like one or two." She said that she'd like them too. Soon, she thought. "Good. So do I. I don't want to be too old to enjoy — we will never tell our children that we nearly had them living in a murder house. All right?"

"Yes, I agree." She smiled at him before continuing. "You're looking better. I think just getting you away from there helped a great deal. As for the place still being used, that's nothing to do with us or any of the rest of the family. If they try any shit with us, I'm a damned good attorney, and I will take on the fucking government if I need to."

Harlin looked at her. She was his love. His first and only true love. Thinking about how his life was going up until meeting her, he couldn't believe how lucky he'd been to find her. Not only that, but he was sure that if his life hadn't changed when it did, he'd not be here today loving her so much.

"I love you so much, Raven Bentley." She told him that she loved him as well. "Good. Now, if you're up for it, how about we go and get some dinner. I'm thinking salad. With some kind of non-red dressing."

They were both still laughing as he put the car

into reverse and started to pull onto the road again. The kids were being gathered up by their parents, and he was enjoying watching them fuss about having to head home. He didn't know why, but he kept his eyes on the little one that was at the top of the jungle gym. Harlin pulled back into the lot and watched the little boy.

He hadn't any idea what had had him watching the kid. He wasn't doing anything wrong. He'd been playing with the other children like the others had, calmly and seemingly nice. But something had caught his attention, and he couldn't shake the feeling that he needed to see what he did next.

All the other children were gone by the time Harlin made his way to the kid. He'd gotten out her wheelchair and had helped her into it before they rolled to the picnic tables not far away. While Harlin hadn't told her what was going on, she kept an eye on the boy. He was sort of eerie. Something about him touched her deep in her soul. And not in a good-feeling sort of way.

He didn't come down off the equipment. Neither of them got too close to him either. As she was resting in her chair, Harlin sat down at the table with her. Neither of them looked at the kid, but she knew that they were very aware of him. And he was of them. When he started off the playground toy, Raven felt herself tense up enough that she was afraid of hurting her leg again.

"Hello." Harlin turned to look at the boy and only nodded. "Can I sit with you? I'm not going to harm you."

If he meant saying that to keep them from being alarmed, he failed. As he stood there, Raven realized that he was far from a boy of ten or twelve like she thought. But more of a man in his early to mid-twenties. He'd shaved today. Or perhaps recently. There wasn't any kind of peachy fuzz on his face or chin. The shirt he had on was larger. She thought it was that way so that he could hide under it. Not just for his age but strength as well. Reaching for Harlin's hand when the man sat down next to where she was gave her very little feeling in the way of safety.

"Are you from around here?" Harlin told him that he'd only just moved here. When the boy man looked at her, she told him that she had grown up here but had been away at work for some time. "You guys own the old Cleary place, don't you?" Raven looked at Harlin, taking her cues from what he said.

"I don't know that name. Like I said, I've only recently come here. Are you from around here?" He said that he'd lived here all his life. Harlin laughed a little. Had she not been looking at the man, she would have missed his show of anger. "You don't look old enough to be using the term all your life. That's more of a line for someone my age. I'd lived in Washington state all my life, and that's a long time."

"You lived around here. Do you know the name Cleary?" Truth. She felt the urge to tell the truth and did. "So you remember the old couple, the Cleary's, I guess. Derick and Annabell Cleary."

"I knew the house, but I never knew their name. If I did, I didn't remember it. Are you related to them?" He asked her again if she had purchased the Cleary home. "No. I didn't buy it. I was here in town helping Mrs. Pastor with her family. I'm sure you might remember them. I did."

"I know who they are. All of them." She nodded and looked around the playpark. Another thing she'd not do was to bring her kids here. Raven thought that she'd talk Caleb into tearing it down and starting again. That would be the only way she felt better. "So you don't live in the Cleary home? The place with the big barn out back? I spend a lot of time there. As a younger kid, I mean."

"Oh really? I've only been in the barn from the front door. But it's massive. I did wonder at one point if it held any of the secrets of the family." Harlin looked at her as he spoke to the man. "We were just by there on the way out of town. There are all kinds of police there. FBI and whatnot. I don't know what's going on, but—"

"Don't move." The gun appeared before she could move. When the man put it to her forehead, she kept her eyes on Harlin. "I want you to explain to me why you two thought to lie to me. I know who you both are. While not your names but you lied when you told me that you didn't own the house. My grandparent's home. Why would you set to piss me off that way?"

"We don't own the house. We only recently got married, and it was going to be gifted to us next week as a wedding gift." Harlin didn't move, but she knew by how tense his hands were with hers that he was going to do something. Whether it was stupid or not, she'd soon find out. Raven loosened her hands that held Harlin's. "My wife and I were by the house and did see the police there. But to be honest with you, we came here to talk about looking for a different home. One that isn't so large."

The pop of the butt of the gun to her forehead made her head swim. Not having time to realize how hard he'd hit her, Harlin moved, knocking the man off the bench and onto the ground. They were both trying to get the gun freed, and she knew that she had to do something. That was when it hit her. She was armed too. She pulled out her weapon and fired at the man on the bottom.

His scream nearly had her telling him that she was sorry. Raven had never shot anyone before. But hitting him in the bottom of his foot gave Harlin just what he needed to subdue the man. And for her to wheel over to them and put the gun to the stranger's head.

"What the fuck was that for? We were just having a nice conversation." She didn't move the gun away from him, even when Harlin pulled out his own and aimed at him. "You two are certifiable. That's what you are. Can't a man just have a nice conversation with —"

"Honey, I've got him. Back away, please?" Harlin had to repeat himself twice before she looked at him. "Raven, I want you to back away from this man but keep your gun on him. If he so much as twitches, I want you to blow his fucking brains out. All right?"

"Yes, all right." She pulled out her cell without looking away from the man. "I'm calling the police. I think we need the police here. Don't you?"

"Yes. You be careful." The man was bitching about how they didn't need to involve the cops. That he was cooperating, and if they would just let him go, he'd not press charges against them for knocking him back. "Shut up." Of course, the man didn't.

He kept getting angrier and angrier as he lay there. Telling them how he'd never see the inside of a jail or prison. Telling them that he'd been at this too long to have someone catch him so unawares that he didn't have a backup plan. Whatever his plan was, she had a feeling that it wasn't going to plan right now.

Harlin was able to get the man's wallet out of his back pocket. When her phone was answered by Doughtery, she'd been given his card while they were at the scene. She told him where they were, what was going on and that both she and Harlin were armed. He said he was on his way.

"His name is Benson Cleary. He's thirty-eight years old, and his address is that of the Cleary home."

Benson kicked out at Harlin to knock his gun away when she fired at him again. This time she hit him in the hand where he'd been raising it with his gun to point it at Harlin. "Good girl. You're the best partner I've ever had, love."

"I love you too." She could hear the sirens as they made their way to the little park they were in. It occurred to her that the Cleary home was nearby, through the park and the next street behind it. Raven was both happy and terrified that they'd stopped there. While neither of them had any proof that this man was still doing the killings, she had a feeling that they'd just captured him. He wouldn't have been old enough to have done the first murders, but she had no doubt whatsoever that he'd been using the barn recently. She'd been an attorney too long to let this opportunity go. Laying her phone down, she put it on record. An app that she'd been using since it first came to her attention that she had it. "Why did you kill all those people? I know you didn't kill them all. And there is no pressure for you to answer me. But since I had planned to live there, I believe that you want to tell me."

Benson laughed. "You think you're so smart, don't you? You think I'm going to answer that? To tell you that I did kill all forty-one people? Not a chance. Unless you beg." This time it was her that laughed. His anger was palatable. "You won't laugh at me when I get out of here. I'm going to hunt you down and cut you into pieces. I'm really good at it too. I can cut down a body in less than twenty minutes. Of course, that doesn't count the time that I play around. Even fucking them before I allow them to die. Did you know that a person's screams can't be heard in that part of the basement? My daddy taught me that. As I'm sure, his daddy taught him. Oh, what fun we'd have down there when there was no one to hear us. Then some asswipe had to build a pretty little playground, and it messed up my killing spree. No one trusts like they used to."

"Isn't that just a shame for you?" She glared at Benson, letting him think that she didn't want to hear anything else. So when he smiled at her again, it took all her willpower not to puke on him. "So you had this nice little family shit going on? How nice for you all to have kept it in the family. I bet your grannie and mom were just thrilled to no end to have all this going on right there in front of them."

"Who do you think lured people to us? Grannie, as you called her, was especially good at it. She'd run a little ad in the paper for a room to rent, and there would be five to seven more deaths that no one would ever know about. Until you two came along." Benson looked at Harlin then. "You should let me go so that I can show you my work. We can have that little missus of yours out of your hair in no time at all. Just let me make some arrangements to have the barn ready, and we'll treat ourselves to the best time you'll ever have."

Raven wasn't worried about Harlin wanting to do anything like that, but she had an idea that Benson was trying to bait him enough that he'd either kill him or approach him. If he did, she didn't know if she would be able to kill him before he hurt the love of her life.

"Nah, I don't think so. I'm liking you right where you are." When Benson started to sit up, Harlin kicked him in the head. "You just stay right where you are, or I will put a bullet in you. I won't kill you, but I will make you fucking hurt. Ah. The police are here. I hope you get the life, several life sentences that you deserve, Benson Cleary."

It didn't take the FBI long to have Benson wrapped up. He not only had on cuffs, but he also had leg irons on, as well as another agent standing

over him with his gun pointed right at his head.
After Caleb showed up with Tabby, she was told that
she had to hand over her weapon. It was the hardest
thing she'd had to do. Hand over her only line of
protection while a monster was sitting on the ground
so close to her. Harlin kept his, however.

"He works for me." No one bothered him after
that. She hadn't realized that Tabby had that kind
of pull, but she was glad for it. Almost as soon as
she was able to relax, she remembered the recording.
While she knew that it would more than likely not
hold up in court, there was a chance, and she wasn't
going to let that go. Handing it over to Doughtery,
the person that seemed to be in charge, she was so
relieved when he began listening to it than she had
at any court hearing that she'd ever won.

Caleb asked them if they'd still have dinner
with them tonight. A celebration, he told them.
Without a second thought, both she and Harlin said
they would. Then she remembered Glenna and that
she was to meet them at the house soon.

"She's at our home. Judge Martin, he was
called in for a records search, and he said that he'd
make sure that she was all right. I think he might
also be questioning her about a job that he has in

mind for her. Did you know that Glenna was a court secretary a long time ago?" Raven said that she had but thought that she'd not enjoyed it. "I don't know if it's Herman or the job, but they seem to be sort of sweet on one another. Now that he's going to be retiring, I think that the two of them could get into some trouble together. I know that I'd like that for the both of them."

"I believe I would as well." As they were waiting on the next round of questions, there seemed to be a lot of people that had a great many questions about how they had spotted Benson. She told all the departments the same thing. "I don't know. It was Harlin first, but the more that I watched the man around the kids—and if you ever tell me that there are children in any of those bags, I'll hurt you. But the more I thought about him and the distance between him and the parents, I realized that he was trying to lure them away. I saw him pointing and gesturing toward the Cleary home before they all left. I was able to take a picture of the kids before they left. It wasn't on purpose, but I was trying to see if I could see our former home from here. Maybe you can contact their parents or something. I don't know. But surely someone will recognize them once you show them off."

"We're also going to have satellite surveillance of the area too once we determine times for some of the killings. He said that his mom and grandparents were in on it as well? You know, that's just sick." She didn't even bother telling him that she thought so as well. They were all sick. "Thank you for this, Raven. If you two need anything, just let my department know. You've been given priority clearance for helping us out on this case."

She was glad that something was going right. All she wanted to do was to find a place to live and sleep for about a month. Whatever went on while she was out, she wasn't going to give it a second of her attention. Raven was finished.

Chapter 5

"I'm not sure what it is you think that I can do, but I'm not going to help you unless you help me. It's not just important to my husband but to the legacy of his mom too." President Davis laughed at her. "I know that you think that I'm teasing you, sir. But I assure you that I'm not. I have means, and while I'd never say what those means are, I think you understand."

Closing her eyes, she waited for the president to speak again. But all he did was laugh. Loud and hard. It did make her smile a bit. Knowing she'd gotten one over on the man and him finding it funny was more than she could have hoped for.

"You've picked up some balls somewhere along the line, haven't you, my dear. Seems like you could have taken some rules that you go by from Abby." He laughed again. "You can call off your man, Yazzie. I'm going to help you."

She sat down hard. Her nerves were frayed right now, and she wasn't sure how much longer her legs could have held her up. He did warn her not to do that again. Even for being blind, she couldn't help but feel good about what she'd been able to do.

"No, I won't have to so long as you know that I mean business when I ask something of you. I've been working for you and the country for a long time. I've never once asked you for anything in all that time." Her head was still spinning. "I honestly didn't think he'd be able to get into your place. Much less been able to pull a gun on you. He did that, right?"

"Yes, he did." She messaged the young woman, glad that the president thought he'd been dealing with a man and told her she could leave. "I'm assuming that you think he won't be caught before he gets out of here."

"He won't." And she knew that now. She'd gotten in, and she had no doubt that she'd get out the same way. "Now, about this favor for me. I need for you to help us find Sebastian Gerald. He's gone like a fart in the wind. No social, no driver's licenses. Nothing for any kind of taxes being paid either. He's just gone."

"Yes, when I got the call from Caleb—who I've been putting off for weeks now—I didn't know how to broach the subject. It's not anything that we need to have out in the open. Not none, at any rate." She asked him what was going on. "Mr. Gerald is a person. He also has a good job, a sister, as you've found out, as well as he works for me. The only way to have him safe, and I do mean he'll need to be protected better than I'm protected, he's gone to ground."

"I see." She really did too. In some of her dealings with reading and translating things for the government, she'd come across such things— "I know him. I mean, I know his name. I've read up on him before."

"I think you have, yes. I didn't know that you'd be with the Anderson family when I found out that you'd translated the conversation that had gone on between him and the country's worse enemy." She said that she hadn't put it together until then. "That's the way spying for your country works, dear. You've not told Joey, I take it. That you've been not just translating old tomes for us but actual conversations between our country and others."

"It never came up. I mean, I wasn't keeping

it from him. And I know that I've done a lot of conversations to date, but this one…his name was Spark. That's all he was called, just Spark." He told her that was it. "The world thinks that he was in on it. However, you and I, we know better. That's why we are having a difficult time finding his sister. Even her name, for that matter. You've had them in hiding since…I think for the last five years."

"Everything he was or she was before that is gone. Erased. There are no fingerprints, no dental records. Anything and everything has been taken out of every system around the world. I would imagine a few pictures of others that bear a great resemblance to them as well too." She told him that he still worked for him. "You're much too smart for things, Yazzie. I'm so very glad that your sister had no idea what you did for us. I can't even begin to explain to you how much I would have hated to have terminated you."

She didn't think that he meant that she'd be fired, either. Like the fart in the wind that she called Sebastian, she'd be gone too. And she was positive that she would have suffered badly. When she reached down to touch her notes, she asked him the next question on the paper.

"Will we be able to find him and bring him here? I'd like to do that, sir. If only for Caleb to talk to him for a bit. I think there isn't a man or woman that loves his family more than he does. It won't matter to him if he couldn't keep in contact with him. Caleb would only want what is best for the man and his sister and to know that they're safe." He was cursing again. Softly so that she'd be the only one that could hear him, but it was enough to know that he was thinking about it. "Damn it, woman. You're as bad, if not worse, than Abby Anderson was. God, I miss that woman. But not as much as I should be with you nearly being her. I'll see what I can—I'm going to need something from you. Some favor that I've been trying to figure out how to make happen for a few days now. It's to do with the Cleary man. Benson. He's going to have to disappear."

"All right." He asked her if she was serious. That she was just going to help him. "I will, but not because you need it. Raven does. She's having horrific nightmares about him. Someone here let it slip that the younger Cleary has been killing children. She can't get that out of her mind that he's going to be set free and will be out on his killing spree again."

"Have you read the reports that I have, Yazzie?

How he and his relatives lured and killed all those people? And the reason why?" She said that she hadn't. "To say they were sadists would have been profoundly inadequate to name them. When the older Clearly, Derick Clearly, married his wife, he learned the trade, they called it from her. She'd been killing off men since she'd been about ten years old. Her family never knew about it from what we've been able to find. But her husband did. Their son did, as well as their grandson. The elder couple would go out to bars and saloons and pick up drunks. According to the diaries that were unearthed in the home, she would lure them away by showing them her naked body with the promise of sex. After a while, they had their son dance for the men. Christ, it makes me sick just to think about it."

"I heard that Benson wasn't a Cleary. That his DNA didn't match those of the other members that lived in the house. Did you hear why?" He told her what he'd heard about him being a Cleary by name only. Her belly lurched up so much that she was sure she was going to be sick for the rest of her life. "So he was cut from his mother's womb before she was killed, then raised as their own. Good Christ, that's fucking horrible."

"That's not even a small part of the things that they're finding in the diaries of the family. I don't know who found them, the books, but we all owe them a great deal for being able to put an end to this." She told him that she'd do what he needed. "I need for you to get me the books."

"I guess you want them destroyed." He didn't answer her, and she just sat there. "There has to be a good reason for you wanting them. How about you tell me what that is, and I'll think about doing it."

"Abby Anderson, Caleb's mom, funded the money for the barn to be repaired after a great storm about five years ago. About the time that Benson started killing. I have a copy of the receipt that she signed, as well as a copy of the letter that Derick Cleary wrote to her asking for the help. There are pictures too that accompanied the letter. " If she hadn't been sitting down, she was sure that she would have fallen to the floor. "It's doubtful that she ever knew about the killings. She would have turned them in had she known. But her name is on the billing that went into the repairs. As well as the money that was used to dig out the basement so that the Clearys would have more room. It's not believed by me that she ever went to the site, but just having her name there will hurt Caleb and Tabby in their endeavors in doing the things that they do for the country."

"I'll get them." She didn't know how or when, but she was going to do it. Abby had gotten her into a school for the blind. Helped her find a job that she could do from anywhere so that she could be a productive part of sociality. Yes, Yazzie thought, she'd get them for the president. "I'll let you know when I have them. I know where they're keeping them."

At least she knew yesterday. Someone was reading the books in order of date and making notes on the names of the people mentioned. There were about four dozen of the books, so she was going to have to plan and plan well. Just as she thought that the conversation was over, the president spoke again.

"Benson is going to be killed by inmates. Sebastian will contact Caleb in a couple of weeks. That's the best that I can do. It'll be up to him to decide his next action. But I will support him in whatever he wants." After telling her that, he hung up the phone.

Yazzie sat there for a long time, listening to the conversation that was being repeated in her head. He was going to do it for her. Not only that, but he was going to make sure that Raven's nightmares were going to end by killing Benson. When she heard the door open and close to the front of the house, she waited for the sound of footsteps to know who it was. As soon as she realized that it was Joey, she called him into the dining room and told him everything that she'd done, including putting a gun to the president's head to prove that she knew just what she was doing.

"I can help you." She told him that she didn't want him to get into trouble. "Honey, no one is going to know. You're smart and know how to get someone in and out of the White House. Getting a few dozen books shouldn't be that big of a deal. The reader is at the hotel that is in town. He's to be there for another few weeks. When he's finished, the books will be stored in an undisclosed place. If he gets to the end of the books, he's going to know. I mean, I'm assuming that Abby's name is going to be mentioned in those later books."

"Yes, I think you might be right on that." She sat still, thinking of everything that could go wrong with this. As soon as she had a plan, she smiled at her husband. "I've got it. It's going to take an army, you know that, don't you? I mean an army of seven."

When he understood what was going to happen,

he smiled at her. "I just love the way your mind works. And having the kids to help unknowingly? Well, I think you're brilliant. When do we do this? Soon, I'm hoping. I want to get to them before they bring in someone else to help him."

"That's the plan." As she told him what she was planning and how it would work—who would ever think a blind woman with five kids would rob someone—he smiled larger. She knew this because she could hear it in his voice how happy he was about how it was going to go. Yazzie loved this man more than she did herself.

~*~

"I don't know what happened. They were just here when I went to the bathroom. I couldn't have been in there for no more than ten minutes." While Agent Sampson didn't know how it was executed, he knew that the beautiful petit blind woman had done it. "She just looked entirely too innocent. His agent was having a meltdown, but the Phillips family was calm and as cool as anyone he'd spoken to before. "Mrs. Phillips came to see me. One of her children needed to use the bathroom. After they hurried in there, she handed me a picnic basket of food. I swear to you, I never left the door nor the little girl in the bathroom unattended. After they left, I went back to my work, thinking about how great the food smelled and the books, every one of them, along with my notes, pens and my briefcase, was just gone. She didn't enter the room. Just that little girl, Madison. And that was so quick, in and out, that there...there are too many books for a kid to leave my room without me seeing she had them. And what is she? Five? Six?"

"She's six. Yet the books aren't here. Are they?" The agent got down on his hands and knees and looked under the bed. In the hour that he'd been there, he'd done that five times. He'd even used his knife on the pillow to tear it apart, looking for the books. "You swear to me that she never entered the room? That none of the kids got around you? Did you hear any kind of noise behind you? Like perhaps a window opening?"

"They don't open." To, he supposed to prove his point, the young agent went to the window and shoved it open. He didn't know who was more shocked, him or the agent, when the glass shattered against his hand as he shoved it outward. "Christ, it's broken."

The feeling that he'd figured out how the books disappeared was short-lived. They didn't have any idea who had taken the books, not without proof. Dustin looked out the window and was dismayed to see that they were fourteen floors up. He knew that, of course, but seeing the distance made the height seem more real. He sat down at the table.

"A ghost then. A ghost of one of the dead came in here and took the books." The kid looks so eager for that to be what happened that Dustin wanted to slap him. "There are no such things as ghosts, you idiot. I was just trying to show you how that's not possible. Not to mention, a ghost wouldn't have been able to carry them either. Because you want to know why?" The kid actually said that he didn't. "*Because they're not fucking real.*"

His head was beginning to hurt. Since he'd gotten the call from the young man over an hour ago, he'd had a nagging headache. Now it was out of control the pain that he was having. Dustin wished that he'd retired six months ago when it was offered to him. Then he'd be blissfully unaware of the shit going on right now.

"That Cleary man. Did you know that he's dead?" The kid, he couldn't for the life of him remember his name and decided that it was going to do either of them any good for him to suddenly remember it now sat down on the messy bed. "He was on his way to the prison to keep him from being found by the public when he and four of the five men that were protecting him were killed. It took them having two of their own killed before they realized that they were being shot at. The agent that had survived said it was like the bullets had a homing device on them, and none of them could get away from the shots. Christ, this is a shit storm that I'm going to have to tell the president about. He's going to want heads to roll over this."

"You said you thought that Mrs. Phillips did it. I agree. She was here with her kids, and she was the only one that came here in all the time that I've been working here." He asked him if he thought that a blind woman with five kids could have gotten by him without him seeing her, picked up the dozens of books, his notes and pens without being able to see a damned thing in the room. Then get by him again, all without the aid of sight. "No. I guess not. But I don't know what else to think. Somebody had to come here and get them."

"If you don't want the entire department, not to mention the president, thinking you've lost your mind. I'd not mention that you think you were robbed by a bunch of kiddies and a blind woman." The kid nodded and said he was right. It wouldn't look good. "You think? Christ, kid, you're sitting there wondering how you can get out of this, and I don't see a single way that either of us is going to be alive enough to get our pensions. Especially me."

His cell phone rang, and he put it on the table when he saw who it was. That's all he needed right now as the president himself calling for an update on the man that is now dead, and all the notes that he and his family had been keeping all this time were gone. He was never ever going to live this down. And he was sure he was going to prison. Picking up the phone, he sent the kid to get him a coffee and a donut. A cliche? Yes, but he was grasping at straws right now.

"Good evening, sir." The first words out of his mouth was asking what had happened to the Cleary man. "There was an ambush. We're thinking that someone got word that he had been caught killing those people, and they, we're thinking that at least three of them took him out. Along with four of our agents that were guarding him."

"Four agents. That's terrible news, Agent Sampson. Terrible." The president was quiet for a time, and Dustin found himself terrified of filling him in on any more information. "I'll expect a full report on this. Do you have any of the shooters? To be honest with you, I don't know that I'd want them caught. But we will. We're the ones that are supposed to keep everyone safe. No matter what they've done. This is just horrible news. I hope you know that."

"It is, sir. And that's not all of it." Dustin filled him in on what had happened in the hotel room. He didn't mention ghosts nor how they had thought that Mrs. Phillips and her kids had been in on it. Dustin knew for a fact that the young woman was a friend of the president. Not only that, but he'd heard that she was working for the government in rereading tomes to be translated. It would be a powerful blow to have to have someone come back on his ass for investigating a blind woman for this. Not to mention a group of children.

"What the hell are you doing down there, Dustin? Running a shit show? Sounds to me like you should have retired years ago. If you can't keep an eye on a bunch of books that will—Christ, it's a good thing that he's dead. It would be difficult, if not impossible, for us to try him now, don't you think?" He only agreed with his boss, sure that if he said anything else, he'd have his badge, his pension as well as spending the rest of his life behind bars. "What am I supposed to tell the country when they find out what the hell is going on down there? What do you think? Should I tell them that since I didn't think it would go badly that I sent my worse agent there to watch over things? I'm sure that will be what they're thinking. Damn it. I want you here on the next flight you can get out. And that boy, Wyeth Forney. He's the one that was going over the books, I'm to understand, correct?"

"Yes, that's his name." He was asked if he hadn't known who the boy was. "No, sir. I mean, yes, I knew his name, but it slipped my mind when I was here working things out on what happened."

"Did you get it figured out?" He said that he hadn't a single clue. "I haven't any idea if that's good or bad right now. Someone out there—maybe I should have hired him instead of the group that is down there. He would have been able to have kept the books safe, I think. Just get here. Today. Christ."

When Wyeth returned with coffees in a cardboard cup and a plate with donuts and another with carrots and celery on it, Dustin bit down on the fattest donut on the plate while the kid munched on the loudest vegetables he'd ever heard.

"We're in deep shit here." He told him that he figured that. "They sent us to the White House. I hope you have all your ducks in a row."

"I don't have any ducks to line up, sir. I just started this job three weeks ago." So much for being a newbie, Dustin thought, they could use some experience around here. "Do you think we're going to be killed?"

"If I were the President of the United States, I would not send two men to appear before me if I had plans to kill them, Wyeth." But if he was honest, he didn't have any idea. "Just keep your mouth shut about Mrs. Phillips and her kids and ghosts and windows and all that other crap unless asked about it directly by someone who is authorized to know what you do. All right? Donuts are good; embrace them as an eternal source of comfort in times of stress. Donuts are life."

They were on the next flight out. The two of them sat side by side, and neither of them said a word to anyone. Neither of them looked even remotely interested in anything around them. And as much as he wanted a drink, something strong and that would knock him out, he didn't order any. He needed to be his best when he got to the White House.

~*~

Wilhelm picked up his private phone and dialed the number he'd called just yesterday. He wouldn't say this to anyone else, but he was impressed. Not just what Yazzie had been able to do for Caleb but that the killer was dead as well. He'd not gotten around to ordering it done. When she answered, he asked Yazzie if she was going to be running for his job.

"No. I think I'd have trouble navigating the oval office. Not too many markers around the room for me to get around. Not to mention getting around the whole building. I am blind, you remember, don't you?" He laughed. But then he turned around to see if anyone was behind him again. "I didn't send anyone to make my point, sir. I think you understand that I'm better than even your best agents. What will happen to them, by the way? Wyeth and Dustin?"

"Christ, you knew who they were too?" She told him that he should never doubt her. "I swear to you, Yazzie, I never will again. As for the two men, they're on their way here now. I'm going to make sure that Dustin retires. He needs to. The poor man has cancer, and it's starting to take hold of his daily life. Besides, I think his wife wants to pamper him a bit. As for young Wyeth, he's going to be just fine too. And as afraid as I think he is about what is going to happen to him, I don't believe that he'll tell a soul about what had happened. I'm going to make sure that the books are gone and that — are they coming to me soon?"

"No. I don't mean that you won't get them, but after talking it over with a couple of people, I think it would be best if they were never in the White House. There are just too many people around that could find them. No, for your own well-being, I have them in a safe place. And when you're out of office, if you still think that I can't keep them safe, then I'll return them to you. If, that is if, you still want them." He told her that he had no doubt that she'd keep them from falling into the wrong hands. "Thank you for that. Three things that I want to tell you. Caleb got a call from a man yesterday that said he was coming. Then he hung up. Nothing else but Caleb is excited to have heard from the mystery man. The second thing is, the playground that Benson was using as a lure to get people to his home is going to be torn out and redone. It would be nice if you were to send a little gift to the grand re-opening when it happens. Also, so I guess I have four things, the house and the barn have been burnt to the ground. A lightning flash caused the barn to catch, and since it was mostly wood, it was too quick for the fire department to stop. And with the winds blowing up while they were trying to save the barn, the house caught too. Sadly it was too much for our small department to handle saving two very old structures at the same time. The good news is Harlin and Raven are being given the insurance for both places, and they're going to buy them something to live in. Caleb wants them to build on the same spot, so we'll see what happens there. He suggested that it would make the ground fresh to have a new start for the ground."

"My dear lady, if you don't run for president someday soon, I'm going to do what Abby did to me. Pick you up, shake you off and steer you in the right direction." She said that she didn't want that job but was enjoying being a mother so much more. "And I bet that you're the best at that too. Maybe you'll talk one of your children into running. I bet with you as their guide, they'll do their country proud."

"Well, of course, they will."

He was still laughing when he closed the connection. He was going to have to sneak down there more often to talk to the family in person. They delighted him in more ways than he'd had with his pretty little wife before she died.

Wilhelm made his way to his home office. After putting his cell away, he sat down at his desk and wondered what his dear friend Abby would have to say about what he'd just done. She'd be happy that he was able to spare her son the trouble of seeing her name associated with a killer. He could almost hear her now.

"It's a right shame that someone has to be going behind you cleaning up messes that were created, don't you think?" He smiled as he thought of her scolding him about being so terrible to two of his agents that hadn't anything to do with what had happened on their watch. He was sure she'd have plenty to say about that too. When his phone rang, he was told that Dustin and Wyeth were on their way to his offices.

"Tell them that I'm much too stressed to talk to them this evening. But I want them here first thing in the morning at seven sharp." The phone operator told him that he'd tell them. "Good. Also, can you get with my staff? As I said, I'm very stressed right now and set up a large breakfast to happen in my rooms with the two agents? I'd like to reem them privately, and having a full belly will make me feel better anyway."

"I can do that, sir. It would be my pleasure. Oh, before I forget, there is a note on the calendar that I have charge of that says that it's Abby's birthday tomorrow. I'm not sure who that is, but would you like for me to arrange for flowers to be sent to her for you? I don't mind, sir." He told her that he'd take care of himself. He needed to do that. "Yes, sir. I understand. Until tomorrow then. Good night sir."

"Good night, Katie." He hung up the phone and went to his room. After getting ready for bed, he microwaved himself some popcorn and put in an old DVD. It was of a party that had been thrown in his honor. The one where he had proposed to Abby, and she gently and politely turned him down.

Chapter 6

"I've been wanting to jump your bones." He looked at Raven, then back at his meal. Taking breaths into his mouth and out his nose slowly wasn't helping like it had since she and he had found a house. Well, the community had helped them find a house, and it was Caleb that helped them buy it. Christ, he was still— "Are you listening to me? I want to have sex with you. Make love. Whatever you want to call it. But I'm trying to figure out how we can make that work with me in this cast from my foot to my thigh. It's making it difficult for a lot of things but sex? I'd like to know if you have a clue how to make that work for us."

"Yes, I did hear you, love." He looked up at her, hoping that she could see the lust in his eyes. Because his body was one hard hormone right now. "Having sex with you or whatever you said—because, to be honest with you, all I heard was that you wanted to jump my bones after that, nothing. But yes, I do have ideas. I can lay you out on this table, and take you against the wall and come deep inside of you. Or even on the couch. I could care less so long as I don't hurt you. Even if you were to sit on my naked cock and ride me. That would be great as well."

She giggled. Smiling at her, he asked her what was funny. "You look like you're in pain. I am too. Not from my injuries but just in lust pain." He stood up so quickly that their new dining room chair fell backward on the floor. "I take it that you might be ready."

"I have been ready since the day that I met you. You've no idea how ready—well, perhaps you do. I ache to have you." She told him that she needed to eat her dinner first. "Are you teasing me right now? I have to tell you, Raven, I'm a man on his last legs here of not just taking you where you sit."

She laughed this time, not just filling him with happiness but also hope. He really was just barely hanging on. When she began eating, he joined her. Harlin thought she might have it right in that they'd need more strength when they had sex. He knew that he was going to use all his pent-up energy just to make her come as many times as he could.

"I've decided a couple of things about this house. If you don't mind us talking about something else." He nodded, not sure what she could be deciding since they'd only just moved in today. "I'd like a pool. If for no other reason than when the family comes over to visit, I want to see the excitement and joy on the faces of the family when they get to swim. I have noticed that they don't do a great deal of swimming but more horsing around—is that a term to use? Anyway, that's one thing. Also, I know that there is a staff house here. Shelia said that she doesn't want to live in it. She said that she has a home that she loves. So what about using it as a home for Glenna?"

"That's a good idea. I've not seen it, have you?" She told him only that she knew that it was one level and had two bedrooms. "Yes. I have the specs on this place. I'm sure that I saw something about it too. Let me get it."

While he went to his office, for now, it was just a table that had a computer on it and a kitchen chair, he found the paperwork right away. He really was going to be working with Tabby and Joey. Right now, he was going to be taking over the duties of

Joey until he was able to get around. The doctors were impressed with the way he was healing. Taking the paperwork to the dining room, he pulled out the sheets on the butler's house for them.

"It has two bedrooms and two bathrooms. It also has a half bath in the garage. I can see that coming in handy." He read through the notes he'd been given. "It says here that there is an eat-in kitchen, a pantry, as well as a laundry room off from the kitchen. That's nice."

"I think so as well. I'll call Glenna tomorrow. She's having so much fun at Joey's home with helping out Yazzie with caring for him and the little ones, she might not come to live with us." He put the paperwork aside and asked her what else she wanted to do. "This house. I know that the kitchen has been updated in the last few years, to which I'm so happy. But I think we need to do a little bit to make it more user-friendly for me. I don't mind cooking, but if possible, I'd rather not. But Shelia is not going to be here on Sundays and only half day on Wednesdays. We'll have to figure something out."

"We can go out both nights if you want." She told him that she was thinking more in line with when he had to work late. "Oh. I guess I will need to be doing that on occasion. Okay, whatever you want to do, go for it. You do remember that we were going to be given some money from the state for finding the Murder Barn." She nodded, and he was glad that she wasn't still having nightmares about that place. "With the house taking care of my mom's expenses now, I can use my pension check from the military for things that we might need as well. We're going to fill out the house, right?"

"Yes. That was another thing that I wanted to talk to you about. The bedrooms." She smiled at him. "I don't know why we thought that we'd be going smaller when Caleb was in charge of helping us find a house. This house had twelve bedrooms and six bathrooms. That is not smaller, in the event you didn't get that."

"Oh, I got it all right. But it was this house, which is too big for us or the mansion down the street that has twenty-four bedrooms. I don't know why he didn't let us pick one of the ones that he owned for the other brothers, but he said that he had something in mind for us. I never dreamed that it would be this one." He looked around the expansive dining room. "I have to admit, between this room and the rest of the house, this one and the living room are by far my favorites. I love all the windows in here. It makes this room look like we could host a great many people here. We will sometimes, but I love this room."

"I do as well. The sunroof—" They both looked up at it. "It's the most wonderful thing to me right now. And the fact that it's reinforced with a special kind of glass makes me happy too. I've seen too many horror movies that have people invading homes that way." He laughed when she did. "Also, not trying to make you want me more, but did you see the master bedroom has a sunroof too? And the windows in there have the most spectacular view ever. I can see us having a lot of deer roaming around back there."

They had five acres. It didn't sound like much, but they had the lot on either side of them. No close neighbors was all he could think about. Then there was the fact that they had an entire acre of wooded land behind the house. That was something that he was looking forward to exploring. He realized that he'd missed something when he looked at Raven. She had a look like she knew that he wasn't paying attention.

"I said that your phone is ringing." She laughed as he fumbled around to pull it out of his pocket. When he was able to get it loose, the person had hung up. Calling back the number that he didn't recognize, he went directly to voice mail. Shaking his head, he put the phone down. "We need to do what the others do when they're eating or have people over. Just put a basket at the front door to put the phones in. We have a house phone. People that want to get in touch with us when it's necessary, they can call us on that."

"Good idea." When his phone rang again, he noticed that he had a voicemail. Answering with his name, he was relieved that it was Martin calling. "I didn't get my phone out of my pocket in time. I'm sorry—"

"You don't have this on speaker, do you? I don't want Raven to hear right now." He said he had to take this and went to his office. While he didn't shut the door, he did get far enough away from it so that he could hear. "Glenna had a massive stroke an hour ago. She didn't make it. She was out back with Joey and Yazzie having a wonderful time, and Joey told me that she just stiffened up and slumped over. She was gone before he could get to her. He said that she had told everyone that she wanted to just go when she went. He didn't do anything to try and bring her back."

"I'm so sorry. Were the kids there?" He said that they were but taking it very well. That they had loved her as much as they all did. "Yes. She was a great woman. We were just talking about where she was going to be staying with us. Raven is going to take this really hard."

"I know. I thought that it would be better coming from you than anyone else. I told the police that you would handle it, telling Raven. Is that all right?" He told him it was perfect. That he would break it to her gently. "I knew that you would. Also, you should know, or perhaps you do, the police, when they arrived, did nothing to resuscitate her either. They had been forewarned as well, they told me. And that she was to be cremated without services. The funeral home will hold off on that until Raven goes by. I guess she has instructions too for her cremation."

"I think they both mentioned it. She has an outfit that she wants to be cremated in. Something about meeting her maker in something fun. I'm going to miss her. She was so funny. I hate to say this, but I'm so happy that she was at Joey's home. She really did love his kids. And being around them, it more than likely made her last day better for her." Martin said that Joey said she'd been laughing, and that was it. "I'm glad. I'll tell Raven that as well."

"I just wanted to let you know before someone else did. You tell Raven that we all love her very much and will be there for her for whatever she needs." Harlin told Martin that he'd tell her and hung up. He sat at his little makeshift desk for a few minutes before going back to the dining room. "Raven—"

"No. I don't want to know. Not now. Later but not now. I know that it was one of your brothers, right?" He nodded. "All right. I don't want to know right now, okay? Just...later. Okay?"

"Yes." She moved from the table and looked up at him from her wheelchair. "I love you so much. How did I get so lucky in finding you?"

"I don't know, but it's me that feels lucky. Every day I love you more and more." He leaned down and kissed her. "How about we go and break in the bedroom. I know that we don't have a bed, but I doubt we could make that work anyway. I need to feel loved by you. Not that I don't, but I need you."

He picked her up in his arms and carried her to the staircase. That was another thing that he loved about this house was the double staircase that led to the upper floors with it branching out to each side of the house at the top. The windows, like their bedroom, had a view of a lifetime to the back yard.

Lying her gently on the floor, she held onto the wall behind her as he stood in front of her. Their bed was coming tomorrow, and their mattress later today. But he didn't want to wait. And he didn't want her to either. As soon as he took off his shirt, he smiled at her.

"I can do this one of a million ways that have been running through my head. I can eat you, which is something that I think we can both enjoy. I can strip you naked and take you hard while the wall takes a beating. Or, and I think you'll like this one the best, is both. Which do you want, my love." She smiled up at him, and he kissed her again. "I love you so much, Raven."

"It was Glenna, wasn't it?" He nodded. "I think you're right. I think that I would enjoy both today. Then later, when the bed comes in, we'll do it all over again on the mattress. Then tomorrow, with it all put together. Breaking in the furniture will be a lot of fun for us both. Don't you think?"

"I like the way you think. Yes, that would be wonderful." He stripped off his pants and boxers, nearly falling over in his haste. He had no idea where they landed because all he could think about was the beauty that was his. When she had her own shirt and shorts off, he nearly cried. He was so happy that she was willing to give this making love with him a shot. "We're going to enjoy this."

Getting to his knees, he licked the long line of cream that was on her leg. Moaning loudly, he looked up at Raven as she stood there with her eyes closed and her body tense. Sliding his fingers up over her knee to her thigh and then into her, she screamed loudly, her body more tense because of her release. Watching her, enjoying her release as much as she did, Harlin pushed his thumb hard over her clit and watched her come a second time.

She was beautiful, but when she came, it was like she'd been shown to him in a different light. That was right, he thought. She glowed. Moving his mouth close to her pussy, he opened her up, pulling her nether lips apart and watched as more of her juices slid down her legs in her need.

Harlin tasted her again. Taking from the source of her, he lapped at her none too gently as he drank deeply of her. Each time she came, he'd lost count already. He was rewarded for his efforts by her flooding his mouth. Juices ran down his chin and onto his legs. This was his best dream come true. To be filled like this with the woman he loved cream.

Lifting her leg that was in the cast, he put it over his shoulder. Not only did he think that it gave him better access to her, but she seemed to lean on him more. As he continued to eat her, feast on her, he fucked her with his fingers, trying not to think about how much he'd love to be doing this with his cock. Then she jerked his head up.

"Fuck me." He told her that he wasn't nearly finished. "You will be if I have to murder you. Fuck me. Hard. I need to feel it to my throat."

Happy to oblige, he stood up. Since he was naked, all he had to do was lift her injured leg up over his hip and plunge forward. Blackness engulfed him. For a few seconds, he didn't know anything other than the pleasure that he was feeling. Coming that hard so quickly had him thinking that when they came together, they were going to move the earth with it. Pausing so that he could breathe around whatever was happening between them, he nearly cried out when one of her hands wrapped around his balls.

Raven grabbed his face with her other hand. She looked deranged but in a sort of lusty way. Every drop of his blood rushed to his cock. His balls ached they were so full. After leaning closer to him and pulling his hair, she kissed him. When she pulled away, still holding onto his hair and balls, she leaned her head against his and spoke. Her voice was ragged and harsh, like just speaking was hurting her.

"More. I need so much more." He kissed her back. "I'm hurting, Harlin. Deep within me. I need for you to make me feel alive again. Like I'm the only person in the world that you will ever touch."

"You are. And you will be." He moved his hands over her body. Cupping her ass, he pulled her closer to him. Her heat and her wetness making his sliding in and out of her so much more delicious. As he pulled her even closer, he smiled. "Hold on, love."

He fucked her. If there had been pictures on the wall, they would have fallen to pieces on the floor. Even taking her as hard as he could, he knew that she wasn't getting enough. Pulling her mouth up to his, Harlin kissed her savagely, tasting blood as he came again. This time with her.

He'd never screamed during sex before, but he did now. Not even as a teenager who was full of shit more than love to Hazel Beckly. When Raven cried out that she was coming again, he could only hold onto her as he fucked her through two more beautiful climaxes until he couldn't hold on any longer and fucked her for himself. Crying out again, he had no chance at all of holding onto his dizziness that sucked him right into a black void.

He didn't know how they ended up on the floor, but he was happy to see that somehow Raven had made it to the air mattress. He didn't move but only to pull the throw rug over his cock and smiled. He'd never in all his life — not ever came as hard nor as many times as he had today.

Sitting up, he looked around the cavernous room and decided that Raven was right. This was a great room. Sitting there, he could see the deer in the woods. Two black squirrels chasing each other around the leaves. It wouldn't be long now before summer was over, and it would be fall again. Getting up, Harlin found a blanket and laid it over Raven, then headed to the shower.

Taking a quick shower made his body less tight. Since Raven was still asleep, he made his way down the long hall. Since their bedroom was the only one that had a view to the back yard other than the staircase, he walked to the end of the hall and started in that room.

Not that he was looking for anything in particular, but he didn't want to have anything in the house that would cause them trouble. He thought that all of them had had enough of that to last several lifetimes.

The first bedroom that he entered was devoid of everything, including any rugs that might have been in the room before. The house, when they'd gotten it, had said as is. The only thing that they'd found so far was that there had been a few pieces of furniture that had been left behind. And of that, they were going to keep.

The room across from that had a large walk-in closet. He wasn't sure why one might need a large closet like this, but he figured that if they didn't use it, they'd be able to change it into something more useful. Then he noticed that there were linens on the lower shelf. A room dedicated to just linens was something that he knew they'd use.

He was in the fifth bedroom when Raven called for him. Since he'd not brought up her wheelchair, he told her that he'd go and get it now. It was a lightweight thing, so getting it to her so that she could get around was no trouble at all. Even when she wanted a nice shower, the shower stall had a nice-sized seat in it that she could use.

"I've been making notes on the bedrooms on this floor. The two on the top floor, the dormer rooms, we can look at some other time. I don't see us filling the house up today." She called to him asking about the bathrooms. "They're very nice. I love that they have both bathtubs—one of them has a claw-footed one and showers. The one with the tub, it has a toilet that is hidden away. I think that would make a perfect girl's bathroom. I don't know why, but I find the tub to be romantic."

"I did, too, when you told me about it." Helping her get dried off, she asked him for some clean clothing. They were living out of suitcases for now, but since they didn't have much, it was working out for them for the moment. "I've been thinking about things. Would you tell me now what you know about Glenna?"

"She was in the yard with the kids and Joey having a wonderful time, Martin told me. Laughing and having a wonderful time. When she suddenly just stiffened up and fell to one side. Not on the ground, I'm sure, but still in the chair. You know which one it is, I'm betting. She loved that old one that Joey had cushioned just for her." She nodded, tears filling her eyes. "She'll be at the funeral home when you are ready to see her. You have something to put with her, he told me when she's cremated."

"Yes. It's silly, I know, but she has this picture of the two of us out to dinner. She was my date at the Attorney Dinner about a year ago. We were all dressed up." He told her that he thought it was great of her to do that for her. "I'll have to contact some people too. They'll need her death certificate before they can cremate her, so I'll need to get—my mind is in overdrive thinking about all the things that I have to do right now."

Picking her up, he held her while he sat in her chair. "Nothing else in this world matters right now but you. If you need for me to do anything to help you with this, I'm here for you. I loved her too. I'm betting that any member of our new family will do the same for you."

He held her for a few minutes, then, when she was ready, he took her down the stairs. Setting her on the only piece of furniture in the living room, an old chair that had been left behind, he took the stairs two at a time to get the chair. When she was in it, they headed out to the car so that he could take her to the funeral home, the first place on her list.

While driving there, she called her boss. After telling him that she would have her resignation as soon as the things were covered for Glenna, Harlin heard him asking her to stay. She turned him down but so gently.

"I've recently married and losing Glenna, it just makes me feel like she was the only one I was meant to help. I will do some things for my new family, but you never have to worry about me and your clients, sir." He could hear the older man laughing. Mr. Palmer told her that it might make his junior attorneys learn something if she did. "Thank you for that. You've been the best, sir."

"You need anything, Raven, you call us. Mrs. Pastor had this firm take care of her will, so when I get the notifications out, you let me know when will work for you. She left you a little something." He didn't look at Raven when she'd been told that, but he knew that she was surprised by it. "If you don't mind, I'll send you the letters of notification for her family directly to you. You have that brother-in-law of yours. Any one of them gets delivered for me."

She told him that she would, and they closed the connection. The rest of the calls were easy enough for her to make, he thought, and when they pulled up in front of the funeral home, he waited while she finished up another call. Then he asked her if she was ready for this.

"I think I am. She had a good life toward the end. And not spending her final day in the nursing home was better than anything. I'm so happy that she wasn't alone when it happened." He told her that he was as well. "I'm ready for this. I know that I'm saying that now and will more than likely break down when I see her, but now I'm ready to go and give her the sendoff she wanted."

He wheeled her into the funeral home and was with her when she saw Glenna. Just as she said, she did break down when she saw Glenna. The funeral director pointed out that she had a smile on her face, the first one that he'd seen on someone in a long time. It was just what Raven needed to hear. He also told her that due to her dying at someone else's house, she would need a full autopsy. To cover everyone's ass. Especially in light of her recent accident involving her children. Harlin and Raven both agreed that was a sound idea.

After having him get her copies of the death certificate when he got his, the two of them left to go to the jail. It was going to be up to her to tell her family that their mom was gone. He thought that she was ready to handle just about anything as she rolled down the hall to the room where they were being gathered.

Donald was the first to arrive. He didn't say anything to them other than he wanted to talk to them when this meeting was finished. Also that he didn't want the others to know. Nodding to him, he told him that he'd do that for him just as he wanted, but there would be no money for him.

"Yes, I'm okay with that." William was next. He was a mess. Whatever he'd been doing, it wasn't suiting him very well. Then the two women. Harlin thought that Donald and William had been sharing a cell but apparently not. The women bitched about being brought to the room since they were napping. He could tell that too. They looked like they'd been on an all-nighter and that they'd been sleeping it off. When Raven looked at him, he cleared his throat.

"I'm sorry to inform you, but your mother passed away about two hours ago. She was enjoying—"

"Hot damn. That's just what I was hoping you'd say." He looked at William when he started whooping it up. "Now we can get this shit taken care of. You're to represent us now, and I don't want to hear any shit about you not being able to. She's dead and gone, and there is no longer any conflict of interest."

"Did you hear what he just said, William Hunter? Momma is dead. Can't you even grieve for her for an hour before you just roll her into a grave and forget about her?" William said he'd not forget her. She was going to make them rich. "I don't care about that. My momma is gone, and the last time we seen her was when you tried to kill off Raven thinking it would get you some money."

"Shut up, you fucking idiot. Not that it matters, I guess, but it's all going to be water under the bridge once we can get out of here now that momma is dead." The women seemed to be agreeing with William. However, it was Donald that seemed to be the most upset. "What the hell is wrong with you now? Whatever she left us, it's going to go to you too. But as the oldest, it's mostly coming to me, if not all of it. I'll make sure you get a cut too."

Donald didn't say a word but sat there crying. The other three were making plans about what they were going to do when they got out of jail. It was William that turned to him, ignoring Raven completely, asking when he thought they'd be released.

"Released? I don't see that happening. You killed a man. Vehicular homicide. You do remember that, don't you?" William waved him off and asked Raven then. "Listen, I don't know why you have it in your head that you're going to be released, but you're not. There are a lot of charges that are against the four of you. In addition to killing the driver, there are the claims about the damage to the limo that Caleb owned. The insurance company also has sued you for you not having insurance when you hit the car. You're not getting out of here."

"Sure we are. Nobody is going to press charges against us on account of us losing our momma. See? That's the way it's going to work. You tell that man who owned the car to get over himself. If he can afford one of those big assed cars, then he can afford to blow it off. My momma is going to make us rich. You'll see that I'm right." When the officer came into the room to take them back to their cell, it was Raven that stopped them from leaving.

"If the autopsy shows that your mother died from anything related to the accident, I'll see you in hell before you can remember your last name. You can count on that." When they were taken away, just as they left, the women first making their plans for the money. Then William telling him to get with Caleb and tell him to back off. He sat down next to Donald when he was the only one left in the room.

"I'm thinking that I don't want to be tried with the rest of them. And if I can, the officer told me that maybe I can press charges against my brother for having us in the car when he killed that man. If he was the one that killed our momma, I want to sue him for that too. I don't like him or the others very much anymore." Raven asked if he'd spoken to an attorney yet. "No. I don't have any money, and I know that I can get me a court one, but I've not done anything about it yet. Do you know someone?"

"I think I might. I'll make a call right now." When she wheeled out of the room, Donald looked at him.

"I don't want to be called Donald James anymore, either. That's a hick-sounding name, and I don't want to be that no more." Harlin told him that he would do that too. "Thank you. I've been talking to one of the policemen here. Well, she's a girl, but she's been visiting me a lot while I'm sitting in my new cell. She's been telling me things too that are going on around town. I know I'm more than likely going to go away for a time. She told me that she'd visit me, but if I can, I'm coming here to stay. Because of all this mess, my wife divorced me and took the kids too. I want to start fresh."

Raven joined him in the room again. Handing her cell to Donald, she told him how Mr. Palmer said he'd represent the young man and he'd be happy to do it. Raven said she was going to send all the paperwork that she could find too. And the police recordings at the scene of the crime.

When Donald handed her the phone back, he was crying again. While he'd not heard what Mr. Palmer had said to Donald, he could see that it gave Donald comfort. Before he was taken back to his cell, he asked if he could say goodbye to his momma. Harlin told him that he'd try and make that happen for him.

Chapter 7

Toby cleaned off the bar while watching the game on the big screen. It was the best seat in the house unless you were at the game, she thought. While she didn't love being a bartender, she did enjoy the perks of it. Games with people she knew. Snacks as much as she wanted and a beer on occasion when it was a great game. The door opened down from her, and she watched as a man walked in and sat at the bar. Making her way toward him, she was surprised at how handsome he was. Not only that, but since he was sitting on a barstool, he was as tall as her six foot one inches.

"What can I get you?" He said a beer and a burger. Well done too. "Fries? Or tater salad. Or both. It's late, so they'll be throwing it out at the end of the shift anyway since it's Saturday."

"Both?" Nodding, she made her way to the kitchen. Sammy said he'd get it right up, and she pulled his beer. They had it on tap so she could watch the game that was going on while she did it. Taking him his beer, he asked her if she knew someone named Anderson. "I'm on my way to finding him around here."

"First or last name?" He grinned and told her last. "There's a couple here named Anderson. They're an older couple."

"No, this guy would be about my age. Late twenties to early thirties. I don't know what he does or what he looks like." Toby didn't know why, but she felt alarms go off in her head. There was no way that this guy was in his late twenties to early thirties. She'd put him more at the top of being in his early fifties. There was graying at his temples, for Christ's sake. "I think he's married, though. Does that help?"

"Can't say that I know anyone that fits that. You can ask around to the others here if you want. But I don't know." Instead of chatting it up as she usually did, she started away. When he grabbed her arm, she looked at his hand on her. "You will remove your hand from me, or I'm going to hurt you."

"For detaining you?" She only nodded but

didn't move. "I want you to tell me all you know about the man that you're lying to me about. He's looking for his half-brother, and you'll tell me what you know. Now, kid or else."

"You don't want to talk to me in that tone, shithead. I'm a good deal smarter and stronger than I look. Remove your hand, or I will. You doing it will save you time in the emergency department." Instead of letting her go, he squeezed just a bit harder. Knowing that she was going to be carrying a bruise for a while, she smiled at him. "You were warned."

By the time the ambulance arrived, she was serving up more beers. The one that the stranger ordered was eaten by Columbus, the old man that sat in the bar only to watch the game with them. The police had arrived not five minutes later. They were usually quick to respond when she called, as she handled most of the rowdy customers when necessary. Officer Bentley, the new guy on the force, was with the second cruiser. He asked her what happened.

"He touched me when I didn't allow it." He looked at the man on the floor and then back at her. "I warned him to let me go. More than I do for other patrons that come in here. But he gave me the jitters.

Also, he threatened me with telling him something about your friend."

"Which one?" She told him, and he asked her what he wanted. "I mean, did he seem the type that—nah, he didn't want money. What did he want, Toby?"

"He was looking for someone that was half-brother to him. He didn't give me a name, but like I said, he gave me the jitters and then threatened me." Again she looked at the man on the floor and then back at him. "I don't give someone a fighting chance to hurt me again. They must have told you that about me."

"They did. But I was just thinking of how much strength it might take a person to remove someone's arm with a hatch. No offense, but someone as slim and small built as you would have to have a hidden strength you don't let someone see." She told him that looks can be deceiving. "They certainly can. I'm going to call my brother. I know you're going to be closing up soon. Can you wait for him?"

"Sure. I'm off tomorrow and Monday. I don't mind waiting around." The game ended with their team winning. Another football game in the pocket.

Soon after that, most of the patrons left,

Columbus leaving her a big tip when he went out the door. The police were talking to them about what had happened. As it turned out, no one knew that she'd dealt with the man until he hit the floor screaming. They still paid little attention to him as their team was in the in-zone.

Caleb showed up about twenty minutes after two. It was then that she noticed that there was a man in the back that hadn't left. When Caleb shook her hand, the man ambled, no other word for it, to where they were standing. It took her less time than it had Caleb to realize that the man could have been his twin.

Once they hugged, big bear hugs like large men were apt to do, she watched as they sobbed over each other. When Harlin was called in, the three of them talked all over each other while they got acquainted. She went to the back room to rotate some stock that she had planned on doing in the morning.

"Toby?" She came out of the walk-in just as Harlin joined her in the back room. It was a quarter past three now, and she was suddenly feeling her long day. "I'm so sorry about this. We got to talking and lost track of time. This is the man that the other man was looking for."

"Yeah, I figured at much." She locked the walk-in up and moved to the front of the bar. "I'm exhausted, so if you guys wouldn't mind saving this until the morning, I'd greatly appreciate it."

"What time is good for you?" She said that she didn't sleep much, so she could be ready around seven-thirty. "How about we meet at my house and — no, that won't work. I don't have any furniture yet. Caleb's home. We'll all meet there and have some breakfast. Is that all right?"

"Yeah, sure. I'll just need an address." He gave it to her, and she made a mental note of it. "Great. I don't know what else I can tell you other than what I already did, but I'll come over."

When they left, she locked up the bar and made her way out to her car. She was surprised to find another car in the lot other than hers and the man that she'd hurt. When someone stepped out, she pulled her gun and nearly fell to the ground when Harlin said it was him.

"Christ, I could have killed you, you fucking idiot. Who gets out of a car in the fucking dark? You don't do that, or someone might put a bullet in your head. Next time think." He laughed and told her how sorry he was. "Yeah, sure. Now why are you here?"

"We wanted to make sure that you were all right when you left." She asked him if she looked like she was unprepared for shit like someone sneaking up on her. He laughed again. "No, as a matter of fact, you look like you could take on the world. But we did want to make sure that you got in your car safely. The police will be coming for the man's car sometime tomorrow. I wanted to let you know that too."

"Thanks. I have a standing order with the police to make sure that any cars left on the lot for more than twenty-four hours they're to be towed." He told her that was a good idea. "Thanks. I do have them on occasion."

"What do you do? I know that you're more than a bartender. You have skills that I've only noticed tonight. You've been in the service, I think." She didn't answer him. "Or not. You don't have to answer. But I will tell you that my sister-in-law and Caleb have connections that can find out almost anything."

"They'll be wasting their time." She nodded toward her car. "I'm out of here. If you think of anything else tonight, just make a note and ask me tomorrow. I'm dead, standing on my feet right now.

And don't sneak up on me again. It will get you dead."

She made her way to her car while he was still laughing. The moron was going to get himself dead if he wasn't careful. Toby noticed that they followed her home too. She did wonder what they'd think about her house. It was fucking huge, but it was all hers.

Going into her home, she didn't bother turning to see if they left. Once she was inside, she kicked off her boots and made her way to the kitchen. As usual, there were sandwiches left in the fridge for her, and she pulled the plate out and ate one of them standing at the counter. When she was finished with the second one, she sat down at the table and read the notes that had been left for her to go over.

"There you are." Toby smiled at Ginger, the cook and chief of her home. "I thought you'd been hurt. Where have you been, young lady? Getting laid, I hope."

"Yes, by six men. It wasn't as fun as I thought it would be." She tsked at her. Then told her what had happened. "I'm having breakfast with Caleb Anderson in the morning. I'm not going to bother going to sleep now, but I'll take a nap when I get home. Have you been waiting up for me? I asked you not to do that."

"I have to keep an eye on you. It was a promise I made, and you know it." Ginger told her that she was sorry. "I shouldn't have said that. But I did make a promise, and I intend to keep it. How much do they know about you, honey?"

"I guess they'll do a background check. They won't find anything, but they'll do it. Other than what I want them to find anyway." Ginger told her that she'd make her some juice. "No, don't do that. I'm going to go and work in my office for a little while. You go back to bed. Since I won't be here, you should sleep in. Maybe have a little fun with Herman when you guys wake up."

"You little turd." She was still laughing when she made her way to her office. Toby was wide awake now and didn't think that she'd even shut her eyes she was so hyped up right now. As she turned on her computer, she thought of what the Andersons would find.

They'd find that her parents were dead, as well as her grandma. Grandda was still around, but he wasn't ready to face the world, he told her since the love of his life was gone. She also knew that they'd find that she was wealthy, but not anything about amounts. It cost her a great deal of money and time to make sure that no one other than her attorney knew her net worth.

There were little things, too, that they'd find out. Like she'd been a child prodigy. But nothing to the extent of how smart she was. Nor would they find out that she had several doctorates, all of them that had served her well over her young life. At only twenty-seven, she was about as educated as anyone could ever be.

Finishing up on her computer, she closed things down and went to her room, the one that she'd been in since she'd been a child and took a shower. After getting dressed, she was out the door at a little after seven. There was a limo in her drive that she didn't recognize but didn't draw her gun, waiting to see who might pop out.

"You were right." She told Harlin that she normally was. "Good to know. But we didn't find out much about you. But Tabby, Caleb's wife, is making another call now, so who knows. Caleb has been making notes since we left you. I have a feeling that you didn't sleep either."

"I don't sleep much." When she got into the

car with him, he told her that he had checked in on the man, his name on his driver's license said he was Richard Weed. She laughed. "So his name is Dick Weed, is it?" It took Harlin a few seconds to get what she said, and he laughed as well.

"I guess I'm too sleep deprived, or I might have gotten that sooner." The drive to the house was smooth. She had a limo as well but rarely rode in it anymore. She much preferred to drive herself. Unless it was something important that she had to attend. "This is what we were able to find on you."

Toby didn't bother taking the sheet of paper. "I know what you were able to find. The rest is personal." He nodded and put the paper on the seat between them. "What's the big deal about knowing anything about me? It's not like we're going to be besties, is it? I mean, I've lived in this town all my life and have never once run into any of you."

"I don't know. Honestly, I have no idea. I think that Caleb wants it because he feels like he owes you. And he did mention and discarded that you could have been with Dick Weed in some way. Like I said, he discarded that idea right away." She didn't bother saying anything because there was nothing to say to him about it. "You have money. And pardon me for saying it, but I'd say that you have a great deal of it."

"I do." Nothing more from either of them on that. "That man, the stranger that is related to the three of you, he's a hard man. Just by the little bit that I saw of him, I'd say that he's got nightmares that even nightmares would have bad dreams about."

"I didn't catch that. But then I was so happy that he'd made it to us." She looked out the window when the limo stopped. "This is Caleb's house. The entire family is here, including my wife, to meet you. Like I said, they're thrilled that you were able to save our brother."

She didn't want to meet the family and didn't think that she had anything to say to a bunch of strangers. But she was here now and was going to make the best of it. It wasn't until she was being introduced to Tabby Anderson that she saw someone that she knew.

"Gracie?" she was engulfed in strong arms in that second. While she was babbling about how long it had been since she'd seen her, Toby just let her. One thing that she remembered about Gracie was that she would wind down soon. "You're married now? That's wonderful."

"I can't believe you're here. I mean, I heard

that your parents were gone. And your grandma. My goodness, you look so much like her. But I think that the last I heard, you were still—" She cut her off. "I'm sorry. I do tend to forget that part."

Toby could tell that everyone was curious, but she nor Gracie would say anything. As they were headed to the big living room—breakfast was still a bit away yet—they talked about the bar incident. She told them the same thing that she'd told the police last night and waited for the questions. There were plenty of those as well.

When they were told that breakfast was ready, they stopped all talk about anything to do with the bar and any business that might have come up. They simply enjoyed the meal and the light conversation. Just as she was finishing up, a little boy came and crawled up on her lap. She was told his name was George. They stared at each other for several seconds before he finally laid his head on her chest and closed his eyes.

"I'm not all that good with kids." Yazzie, his mother, said that he wasn't all that good with adults other than family. "I'm not family. Why did he pick me?"

"I'm sure that he saw something in you that

he wanted to help you with. I've noticed that about him. He is quick to come to someone when they need a hug." She didn't think that she needed a hug but didn't say anything. "If you're ready, we can tell you what we've been able to find out about Dick Weed."

~*~

Sebastian watched the woman as she spoke to the others. He'd noticed when he'd seen her last night that she was comfortable with herself. In her own skin, he'd heard people say. Not only that, but he was also able to tell that she'd not felt any remorse about killing Dick either. He had died last night from blood loss.

"You said that you lived here all your life. How come we never crossed paths before this?" She asked Caleb if he meant because they were in the same social circles. "No. I didn't mean that at all. I've lived here for less than a year now, and I doubt very much there has been an occasion for us to be at anything that would have social standards. You need to get the chip off your shoulder and let us be friends."

"No offense, Caleb, but I'm not good around people either. That's why I have the bar. My therapist told me that I needed to get better at socializing. I'm not any better after four years." It was him that asked her if she'd had a lot of therapy. "More than most. I've had a — I guess you could call it a tragic life. Not only have I had a lot of death and mayhem in my life, but it's something that I don't share either."

"Toby saw her parents killed. Her grannie too." She looked at Gracie when she spoke. "You're not a terrible person, Toby. But they should know that there is a reason for you being the way that you are. I promise you that no one here will judge you."

"Perhaps not, Gracie, but it was my story to tell if I wanted it." When she stood up, so did Gracie. Sebastian did as well. "What are you going to do? Hurt me?"

"No. I think that you've been hurt more than anyone I know. No, I don't want to hurt you, but I do believe that you need a good friend." She said she wasn't good with people. "You used to be. You used to be as lively as anyone that we knew. Then you witnessed horrific murders, and it changed you. Come back to me."

"I can't." She turned to leave, and he stepped in front of her. He had no idea what possessed him to do that. He'd seen her in action before. "What do you want?"

"My name is Sebastian Gerald. I, too, have

witnessed things that haunt me. My wife and my child were murdered one night. I survived so that I could testify against the men that had done it to them. When I woke up from my coma, my life was forever changed. My wife and daughter had been gone and buried for two years by then. My grandma suffered for a month before someone helped her along by going back to the hospital and murdering her too. I testified against Parker Roman. The boss mobster that wanted me to work for him, and I turned him down."

"He is still out there. You were put in protective custody, given a new name, an identity that they found out about." He nodded at her. "You disappeared. That's why Dick was trying to find you. He knew that you were on your way here. They won't stop, you know this, right?"

"I do. But when I heard from Wilhelm that my brother was looking for me, I told myself that this was a good way to end all of this. This hiding out. Not doing anything that I want to do. Like being with my little sister." She told him, not asked, that he'd changed his mind. "I have. I don't know why that only after a few hours, I've felt better than I have in a very long time. It's a feeling that I'm sure you're unfamiliar with, as I was. But being here, being with this family, gives me more hope than I've had in a good long time."

"I'm happy for you, but what does that have to do with me?" Before he could tell her, she sat down in the chair that she'd just vacated. "They'll come for me now that I've killed one…his name was Roman as well, I'm betting. I'm a dead man."

"We both are." She sat in the chair for several minutes. The others had left them there, and he was glad for it. Sebastian had already told them more than he'd wanted. It had taken nothing for him to share it, either. "I'll help you against them. I've learned a few things myself since I've been out of the hospital."

"I'm a green beret. Special forces, as well as a part-time marshal. I've learned from the best." He nodded, knowing on some level that he didn't get all the information that she'd been trained to do. "What makes you think that I want to live any more than you did before coming here."

"I can see it in your face that you've had enough." She glared at him. "I've got a sister, remember? That doesn't hurt me."

"I don't want to…" She stood up, and he did again. "I'm going home. I think you have enough to deal with without me being here. I can almost feel the questions that they have for you."

"Don't. Please don't leave yet." She headed to the door. "Please, Toby. I've nothing to say to you to hold you here, but I will tell you that I've never felt so helpless until I met you. I feel that. I know that you're not going to like this, but I feel better with you around. Like you could be my rock when I need it."

"I don't want to be anyone's rock, Sebastian. I have enough shit going on right now to fill up several needy bags." He laughed. Sebastian hadn't had a reason to laugh in a very long time. "You think I'm funny that I have baggage?"

"No. I don't think you're funny at all. But I do think it's funny how you described it. Needy bags? I like that." He put his hands up to hold her, but she took a step back. "I think I should have remembered that from last night. But I'm asking you, as a desperate man in a house full of people that want to help me, to please help me by staying."

She looked at the door and then back at him. Toby didn't say anything, but she was thinking. Not that he'd ever play poker or any other game of chance with her, but he knew that she was weighing her options. When she told him that she didn't want to be his friend, a little part of him hurt. But he nodded.

"I have a home near here. Do you think that we could go there for a little while? I need to chill out. To hit the bag." He asked her if that was going to be him. "No, dumbass, a punching bag. It's been a hard day for me. You too, I guess, but I'm not concerned about your pity party right now."

After telling Caleb that they'd be back — at least he hoped so — the two of them got into the limo and headed back to her home. Christ, he thought when they pulled in the beautifully maintained drive, she really did have some money.

True to her word, she went upstairs to change. When she returned, with him a pair of trainers and a shirt, she made her way to the basement. The entire room that they entered was filled with the kind of equipment that would keep anyone in shape. Toby went to the heavy bag and began working it. Once he was changed into the too-large pants, he sat down at a state-of-the-art rowing machine. Hell, he thought, he'd live here with her if only he could use her gym. It was better than anything he'd ever used in most places before.

Rowing relaxed him. He also built up a good sweat. When he'd rowed about as much as he could, he went to the treadmill. Sebastian noticed that Toby was now on the rowing machine, and he was happy that he remembered to wipe it down when he was finished. After about two hours, she told him she was going to take a shower and that he was fine to join her.

"Is there any kind of sensor from your head to your mouth? I mean, you just asked me to join you in a shower." She told him that if he tried anything, she knew how to take care of herself. "Of that, I have no doubt."

He did join her in the shower and found that there was nothing sexual about it. He saw her scars, there were plenty of them, and she saw his. There weren't as many on his body, but hers were hatchet marks and other sharp-bladed marks, while his were bullet holes. When they were finished up, she asked him to lunch.

They were getting along fine, he thought, but they weren't talking about anything serious. He doubted that they would either. When lunch was finished. The two of them got dressed again and headed back to Calebs. He felt so much better about dealing with all of them—he was used to being alone than he had before. Sebastian would have to remember that. To hit the gym when he was feeling overwhelmed again. It had worked wonders on his mind and body.

Kathi Barton, a winner of the Pinnacle Book Achievement Award and a best-selling author on Amazon and All Romance books, lives in Nashport, Ohio, with her husband, Paul. When not creating new worlds and romance, Kathi and her husband enjoy camping and going to auctions. She can also be seen at county fairs with her husband, an artist and potter.

Her muse, a cross between Jimmy Stewart and Hugh Jackman, brings her stories to life for her readers in a way that has them coming back time and again for more. Her favorite genre is paranormal romance, with a great deal of spice. You can visit Kathi online and drop her an email if you'd like. She loves hearing from her fans. aaronskiss@gmail.com.

Follow Kathi on her blog: http://kathisbartonauthor. blogspot.com/

www.ingramcontent.com/pod-product-compliance
Lightning Source LLC
Chambersburg PA
CBHW030226180626
46810CB00008B/2998